*V*OICES OF THE *S*OUTH

The Long, Long Love

ALSO BY WALTER SULLIVAN

FICTION
Sojourn of a Stranger
A Time to Dance

LITERARY CRITICISM
Death by Melancholy: Essays on Modern Southern Fiction
A Requiem for the Renascence: The State of Fiction in the Modern South
In Praise of Blood Sports and Other Essays

MEMOIR
Allen Tate: A Recollection

AS EDITOR
Band of Prophets (with William C. Havard)
The War the Women Lived: Voices from the Confederate South

TEXTBOOK
Writing from the Inside (with George Core)

WALTER SULLIVAN *The*

Long,

Long Love

Louisiana State University Press   Baton Rouge

Copyright © 1959, 1987 by Walter Sullivan
Originally published by Henry Holt and Company
LSU Press edition published 1999 by arrangement with the author
All rights reserved
Manufactured in the United States of America
08 07 06 05 04 03 02 01 00 99
5 4 3 2 1

Library of Congress Cataloging-in-Publication Data
Sullivan, Walter, 1924–
    The long, long love / Walter Sullivan. — LSU Press ed.
      p.   cm.
   ISBN 0-8071-2448-6 (paper : alk. paper)
   I. Title.
  PS3569.U3593L6   1999
  813'.54—dc21
                                            99-31905
                                                  CIP

The paper in this book meets the guidelines for permanence and durability of the Committee on Production Guidelines for Book Longevity of the Council on Library Resources. ∞

FOR MY MOTHER

'O where have you been my long, long love,
    This long seven years and mair?'
'O I'm come to seek my former vows
    Ye granted me before.'

THE DAEMON LOVER

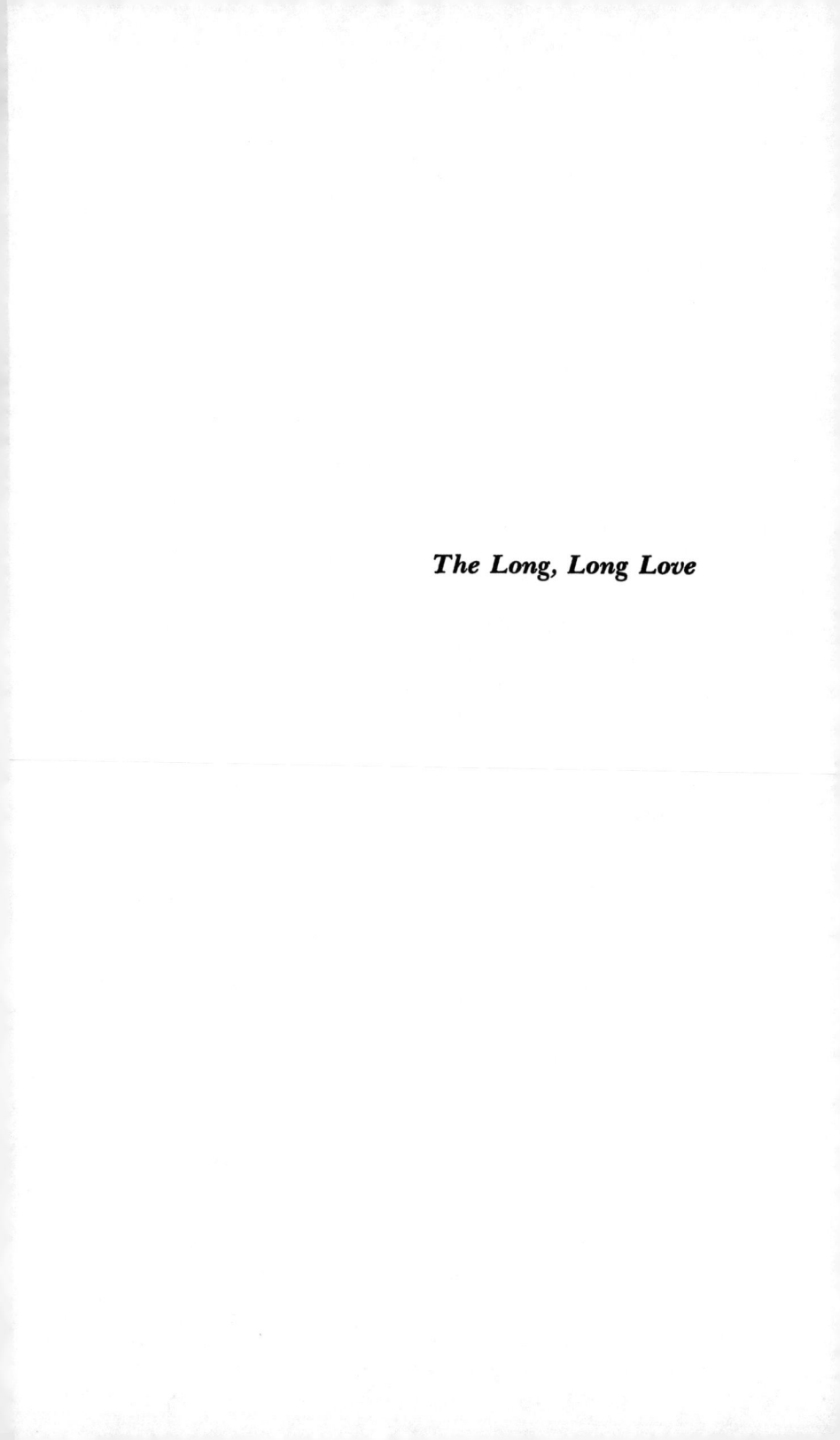

The Long, Long Love

1
The Life and Times of Horatio Adams

I CAN REMEMBER very distinctly that when I was a child, I used to think often about life and about how I came to be where I was, doing whatever I was doing at a particular moment of the day or of the night. My family lived in a house on Russell Street in a section of Nashville that was then known as Edgefield; and it was a big house, three stories with turrets at the corners and as fancy as a river steamer with curlicues and gingerbread and stained glass transoms. Sometimes, if the day were dull, or if my only sister who is dead now had hurt my feelings, or if one of the servants had scolded me for being underfoot, I would climb up to one of the turret rooms—which was round as I imagined a dungeon room would be and dark with only a slit of sunlight through the narrow window and dusty from the desuetude of long years. I would sit down near the doorway—on a stool that I, in my vanity, had provided for myself as a kind of throne to sulk on—and I would listen to the coo of the pigeons that nested beneath the parapet or, if it were summer, to the sough and whir of the circling flies.

But I can truly say that I was not the type of child to pout for very long. Even now, after almost half a century, I can recollect how my mind would inevitably be diverted from the hurt or grudge it bore by a flight of fancy, by a cast of my imagination over the intricate connections that form the fabric of man's days. I would sit with my back against the wall, my eyes toward the window, my hands in my lap. And I would think, *I am Horatio Adams and I am nine years old and I have come upstairs because I am angry with Sister.* And then I would think, *But suppose I had left home right after luncheon to go fishing maybe with Wash Hamilton or to walk to town or down to the park where we might have played baseball. Then I would never have quarreled with Sister and I would not be here now. Or suppose I had been born before Sister, rather than after, then I would be her older brother, larger and wiser than she and she would not dare dispute me. Or, going back further, suppose Mother and Father had not married each other, would I be Father's son now or Mother's and in what ways would I be different and in what ways would I be the same?*

I tried, of course, to keep these thoughts carefully secret; knowingly, I disclosed them neither to my family nor to my friends. Yet my resolution was callow and the mark of its imperfection was the occasional question which I blurted out to Wash Hamilton or to Henry, our houseboy, or to my Aunt Irene. Once I asked Aunt Irene what she thought I would be like and what I would be doing if I had been born in Ohio rather than in Tennessee. My aunt was my father's sister, a tall woman with a sharp nose, who wore black dresses. She was an officer in the U. D. C. and her father had been a general in the Confederate Army; and she was very proud of the South and of herself for being a Southerner and of Grandfather Adams who had given his life for the Southern cause.

"Ohio!" she said when I asked her my question. "Ohio!" she repeated, her voice rising sharply. "Imp of Satan, don't you know where Ohio is?"

So I climbed, pouting, to my turret room and spent half an hour of a bright fall afternoon thinking of Ohio where I had never been and of how the days of my life might have fashioned themselves if I had been born there.

My aunt often said that I thought too much about myself.

And perhaps she was right. At least I know that I had an intractable mind, an imagination which refused sometimes to accept life's reality. For example, Father and Mother went down on the *Titanic* and, although their deaths were definitely established and a memorial service was held for them at St. Ann's Church, for a long time I could not bring myself to believe that they were gone. For two weeks after we heard that they were dead, I firmly expected to see them come home, to arrive in a carriage and move up the walk and across the porch and into the house together. But when the carriage did arrive, it brought my Aunt Irene and my Uncle Billy who had come to take Sister and me to their own house on the other side of town.

I was in the drawing room, that vast, high-ceilinged

parlor with sliding doors and Victorian furniture, a figured carpet, red velvet draperies, and lampshades hung with little red velvet balls. I was dressed and waiting, my face clean, my cravat neatly knotted, when I heard the horses along the cobblestones. I ran to the window and pressed my nose against the glass. It was just at twilight. They had waited until Uncle Billy's working day was over before starting out to fetch Sister and me and now the carriage that stood at the curb was only faintly visible in the first deliquescent half-light of evening. At that instant, my fanciful desire became for me a certainty, and I believed the carriage to be a hack and the occupants to be my mother and father, home at last from their vacation across the sea. Then the cab door opened and a figure descended. Showing in silhouette against the carriage lamp, the figure was that of my Uncle Billy who was short and fat and whose round head sat like a cunningly balanced ball on his sloping shoulders. I turned back toward the room and a few seconds later I greeted my aunt and her husband with my tears.

I left the parlor on the pretense of helping Henry with my baggage. But I went instead to the top of the house, to the turret room where I struck a match and lighted the gas jet and sat down on my stool. I sat and for a moment it was the same. The feeling that I had was the same feeling that I had always had in this room. And then suddenly, it was not the same; it was different and I knew it would never be the same again. For on those other times, when my feelings were hurt or when I was angry with a playmate or a member of my family—then, I could wonder how I got to be Horatio Adams in the first place and I could speculate on what curious and different turns my life might have taken, if this or that event in the past had been changed. And when I wondered what might have happened to me if my mother and father had never married or what I would have been like if I had been born in Ohio, I was denying, for an instant at least, that I really was Horatio Adams and that I had to keep on being Horatio Adams and that I had to accept whatever was meant to happen to me.

Now, I could not deny being who I was. Now, I could not make myself wonder what I might have been doing if Mother and Father had never gone to England, or if the iceberg had never formed in the sea lane, or if the ship that was supposed to be unsinkable had not sunk. I could not think of these things because, as a result of grief perhaps or shock or maybe simple surprise, I was contained, sequestered by the immutable fact of my own identity. And suddenly, in a vague way at least, I knew the meaning of time. I knew that my parents were dead and that on this earth I would never see them again. And I knew that I would never again be able to escape from myself or from the terms of my own destiny by dreams and flights of fantasy and fancy. And I felt, as you seldom feel when you are young, the rush of the turning, orbiting globe, the deprivation wrought by each passing day and hour. Twelve of my years of life were gone. And I saw now, in the fact of my parents' death, both the proof and the harbinger of my own mortality.

I did not cry. My eyes burned drily in their sockets and I sat with my fists doubled up and my teeth clenched, until I was startled by a loud voice which spoke from the doorway.

"I told you he would be here," my aunt said. "I told you he would be up here woolgathering. He comes up here to think about himself."

Father had been very wealthy, richer I think, than even Uncle Billy and Aunt Irene had suspected. So there was no reason for the administrators of the estate to insist that the house on Russell Street be sold or rented. It was left intact. Dust covers were put on the furniture and Henry, who was getting up in years now, was retained to sleep there and guard the house and to keep it clean. At odd times during the summer and at other vacation periods when I was home from prep school or college, I would go from my uncle's place on West End Avenue across town to the house where once I had lived with my mother and father. After I had exchanged a few pleasantries with Henry, I would sit in the library or in the front parlor and watch the play of firelight on the polished andirons or, if the weather were warm, sip a cool drink and fan myself with my hat. I would remember the old time and how it used to be when I lived here and I would think of my mother and father who had died at sea.

Because it seemed to me that I owed them this much. It seemed somehow unnatural, not that they should die, but that all trace and memory of them should be so completely obliterated. Their bones drifted somewhere in the ocean, washed by what water no man could tell. Beyond a memorial window in the church on Woodland Street, there was nothing but this house—no monument to mark a final resting place, no grave where I might have placed a wreath of flowers. I grieved for my mother and father who were lost to the world of man. And I suppose I was aware, in some childish way, that my own life would have to end. I suppose, in a way, I was grieving for myself.

Yet, there was a comfort too in going to this house and conjuring up these images of the past. For after all, wasn't my memory of my parents a kind of monument to them, or better than a monument, emanating as it did from flesh and not from marble? And was not the fact that I cherished the recollection of Mother and Father a promise of sorts that in the future someone, perhaps yet unborn, would remember me?

I loved the house on Russell Street. And attenuated, devoted as I was to the shrines and relics of the past, I loved Adams' Rest perhaps even more. Adams' Rest was a part of my inheritance; a house thirty miles south of Nashville, a farm, a plantation really, on the outskirts of a little town called Van Buren, which had been built by my great-grandfather in 1821. It was a large house, red brick and white columns, and it sat on the top of a little eminence with a vast lawn that sloped gently toward the road. The land was under cultivation: tobacco and corn and pasture and orchards. There was stock in the stables and there were hands to work the fields and there was a skeleton house staff who took care of Uncle Billy and me when we went there to hunt quail or dove in the autumn.

The house at Adams' Rest was full of mementoes. The old ledger books from slavery days still lined the office shelves; the old tester beds remained in the bedrooms; and many of the windows were glazed with the old, greenish, bubbly, shimmering panes. The wardrobes contained relics of a romantic nature: there was a Freemason's apron and an old militia uniform, there were some dresses with hoop skirts and some military belts and an empty holster. On the walls there were portraits of my forebears, of my great-grandfather who had built Adams' Rest and who was now buried in the cemetery beyond the house and of my grandfather who had been a general and a hero and who was buried in town in the Confederate graveyard.

According to the story that Aunt Irene told me, Grandfather had been killed in the Battle of Van Buren and had died almost on his own doorstep; but because he wished it with his final breath or because somebody thought he would have wished it or because the people who had seen the battle and considered him a hero thought it proper— for some reason that was not then entirely clear to me, Grandfather was buried beside his fallen men and after the War, his grave was marked with a shaft of marble. This, I believed, was the finest of all victories over death, the antidote to the depredations of time. Occasionally when I stood alone in the plot, reading the inscription of my grandfather's tomb, tears would sting my eyes and blur my vision. I would look at my grandfather's grave and cry. Such was the callowness of my sentient youth. Oh such, indeed, was my ignorance and folly!

Foolish was I, for of what use was fame, and how could it heal the broken heart or revivify the decaying flesh ere the day of judgement? But worse than this was the belief that the sight of Grandfather's tomb had led me into: that death, your own death, was the worst that time could do, the ultimate pain that the passing years could make you suffer.

My sister died of influenza during the epidemic of 1918 and I, too, contracted influenza that year and I was very much frightened. I remember more clearly than the aches and chills the great silence that would come over the house when Aunt Irene and Uncle Billy had gone to bed, and the nurse who was caring for me had left the room, and I was alone with only the wind beyond the glass, and inside, the night light's steady burning. I did not expect to live and I did not want to die, and many times during many nights I was frightened almost to the point of calling out that the nurse might come or Aunt Irene and hold my hand and touch cool fingers to my forehead. But I did not call out and, when I was well again, I recollected my behavior with pride. From that moment I believed that I, like Grandfather, was capable of dying bravely. I took comfort and—I must admit it—pride in the fortitude with which I had faced up to death. I congratulated myself on what I fancied to be my consummate courage.

And, indeed, in such a fashion are we all deluded, day by day. Men speak of the value of experience: the efficacy of experience brought to bear to solve life's problems, the comfort of experience which whispers that the worst must pass. But this is not true. Experience is a myth for men to cling to. It offers us too little. It is understood too late. The lessons that it teaches are often contradictory.

I emerged from my siege of influenza believing that I had faced up to the experience of death and that I knew now all that there was to know about dying. I had forgotten the lessons I had learned—no matter how vaguely learned—when, as a child, I hid myself in my turret room. I graduated from college. I went to work—if you can call it that, if I have ever worked—in a brokerage firm which had been founded by my father and which was being operated by the trustees for the beneficiary of the estate, who was I.

And one weekend in April when I should have been at the office, I was off at a house party near Lexington, Kentucky. There I met a girl named Nancy Henderson. I remember that on Saturday afternoon we had all been drinking a good deal. Everyone at the party had been drinking too much and Nancy Henderson and I decided to take a walk to clear our heads with the fresh air of April. We were at a farm which belonged to a college friend of mine and from the side veranda, we followed a flagstone path which was lined with iris just coming into flower. I remember how the sunlight caught the purple petals, glowed there softly and glowed on the soft new grass. And I recollect how we moved together—the slight, almost delicate girl and I—walked unsteadily hand and hand to a wrought iron bench that sat by a drained lily pool. We lighted cigarettes and I think we laughed about nothing; laughed in amazement, the way people who have been drinking will do, at the fact that the pool was bone dry now. We got up and walked around in the pool, hilariously pretending, I suppose, that like Our Lord we walked upon the water.

When we had resumed our places on the wrought iron bench, I looked at her for the first time in the full light of day or looked at her perhaps in the first stages of my returning sobriety, but looked at her, in any event, closely. I saw the dark hair cut short as was then the fashion; the very white skin; the face slender so that the features were almost, but not quite, sharp; and below the face, the limbs slender but not too skinny; the legs and arms fleshed out over the small bones to the bare point of a superb adequacy; the calves tapered to suit the eye but strong to carry the light body with grace. And at the same time, at the moment that I recognized her for the beautiful girl that she was, I heard in her voice the Northern accent.

At this distance, I cannot tell you what she said, though I recall distinctly the deep green of her dress, the glitter of a ring on her right hand, the snuff brown color of her pointed-toed, polished slippers. I recollect only the sudden strangeness of those sharply pronounced i's, the finality of the clearly enunciated r's coming at the end of a word or the close of a sentence. I listened for a while in bemused fascination. Then I said, "Nancy, where are you from?"

It was a rude thing to say, an ill-bred question to ask, but I did ask it and she did not seem to mind.

She smiled and said, "Cleveland. I live in Cleveland, Ohio. I was born there."

And oh, how the memories came rushing back of the days when I used to wonder what I would be like if I had been born not in Tennessee, but in Ohio. I remembered my Aunt Irene and how she had frowned and called me Satan's Imp, and my grandfather buried beneath his marble shaft, who for all I knew might have been killed by a man from Cleveland, Ohio. And perhaps even then I had made up my mind to marry this Yankee girl if she would have me.

At any rate, six months later, we were married in Cleveland, and we returned after Christmas to take up our lives in Tennessee. And was it the sight of Nashville and the old landmarks that turned my mind back to its familiar track and started from their slumber the ancient fears of my heart? I do not know; I cannot answer. I can only say that during all the long journey that Nancy and I took together, by ship and rail and carriage sometimes, up mountain and down into valley, through good weather and beautiful country and through snow and rain, during the months of our honeymoon, I felt nothing but happiness. The old depression which I used to feel did not come to haunt me or to suggest that time was passing, that even then fate was planning an end to our bliss. But when we got home and I once more discovered Nancy's beauty, tears came to my eyes.

Before our marriage, Nancy had come down to Nashville on a visit and we had purchased a lot of ground in Belle Meade and had plans drawn up and called in the builders. Nancy had consulted a decorator and hired servants, so when we returned from Europe we were met at the railroad station and taken to a house already furnished and staffed and waiting there bright and new against our occupancy.

We went through our house and admired its rooms. Nancy rejoiced in the richness of its carpets and draperies, caviled only slightly at the arrangement of the furniture. Then we returned to the foyer and went up the stairs to our bedroom suite where fires had been lighted. I remember that some of our baggage had already come out from the station and Nancy's maid was busy unpacking one of the trunks. We sat down in the sitting room, close together on a small couch, and in silence, we watched the play of shadows on the hearth. Then it occurred to me that this was our first time together in our own home and we ought to celebrate somehow. I rang for the butler and asked him to bring champagne.

It was afternoon of a cold January day. The yellow January sun sparkled at the windows and the glass of the windows was misting slightly, and inside was all warmth with the heat of the open fireplace and the house new and clean and very silent. The maid had gone now out of the dressing room and Nancy was beside me, her shoes off and her legs pulled up beneath her on the couch. I released her hand which I had been holding and put my arm around her shoulder and it was as if I had never been close to her, never touched her before. It was as if this were the first time, not only of marriage, but the first moment of courtship. The arm that I felt beneath the cloth of her dress was strange, mysterious in its slender shape and firmness, but tempting far beyond its simple mystery.

I moved closer to her, but I did not kiss her at once. I held off, my lips so near hers that I could feel the warmth and dampness of her breath against my face, and then I did kiss her gently on the corner of the mouth, easily as old people kiss or as you kiss a child. I drew back and kissed her again, and this time it was a lover's kiss. Her lips were as warm and as damp as had been her breath and the breath of her very life was present in our kiss, shaping it, and shaping our lips together. I put my hand beneath her dress and let it brush up along her thigh past the top of her stocking.

"Not here, darling," she said.

I smiled and said, "No. Not here."

I got up and I helped Nancy to rise, and I walked with her through the door into the bedroom.

When it was over—and it did not last long, so great was our passion, so violent was our act—we lay for a while very still beneath the covers, very warm beside each other in our bed. I lay and looked up at the white ceiling, growing dim now in the fading winter daylight, and thought how wonderful it was to be married at all and how very wonderful it was to be married to Nancy. To have her beside me with her leg next to mine, with the muscles relaxed now and the blood subsiding, but the touch of the flesh welcome none the less. Our legs together in the darkness beneath the sheet and blanket, her head on my shoulder, the fine, black hair of her head against my cheek.

But it did not come quite yet, my vision of despair. In full happiness, we rose and returned to the sitting room; naked still both of us, except for our robes and slippers and sat down again by the fire to drink champagne. The twilight was upon us. The sun was setting behind gray winter clouds, the light failing without color; beyond the room, the cold world growing dim. Nancy sat, her hair still rumpled slightly from our pleasure, her head turned slightly away from the hearth glow, so that I could see the curve of her pale neck, the features delicate, but not sharp, the line of the eyebrow above the half-closed, pensive eye. With the glass in her hand, her legs crossed, her robe open to show the slipper hanging off her foot, the bare calf, the half-bent knee, she sat as motionless as a statue, as still as death.

And did I then hear a clock strike or like the poet catch the sound of time's rattle and rush or feel on my cheek the cold and clammy breath? I do not think so, for her beauty was enough. I loved her and I was struck with her physical perfection, beyond all thought of lust or design of passion. She moved. She swung the bare leg gently back and forth, she lifted the glass slowly toward her lips, and suddenly the fear of knowledge clutched my heart. For, oh, she could not always be this way. It could not last, this image of the eye's fulfillment; this beauty, against the days and years to come, could not endure. I saw in her handsomeness and youthful grace the prelude to a terrible loss, the condition attendant before a wrenching disappointment. For the hair would gray, the flesh would sag, youth and its pretty bloom would pass, diminish in the passing hour's sands. Beauty's doom seemed to me then to doom my heart to perpetual bereavement.

That is what I thought and tears filled my eyes.

That is what I did to myself, what I did to Nancy.

For was not this the beginning? Did this not set the tone of our lives, establish, in its mild and seemingly innocuous way, the pattern that our coming days were to follow? I know that taken singly the moments of life are short, the events insignificant, and we turn the eye backward to fragmented recollections. We look backward at this event or that, the bright day, the moon-drenched night, the evening's happiness or the morning's sorrow; and each image, each memory, is whole unto itself, circumscribed, sequestered from the others. But it is not that way. Look backward at birth which should be a beginning but it is not, with the marriage and the night of love before and afterward the christening and the confirmation. And so it is, turn where you will, the times of man's life meld into one another. This is the meaning of the riddle of the sphinx—from the creeping baby to the old man with a cane, it is all one. The present leans toward the breath of the hopeful future and the past lives on beyond its own finality, it transcends the cold embrace of the final earth.

Or perhaps I should put it this way—one remembers what he believes he has forgotten. In the early years of our marriage, when Nancy was taken up with her Junior League and the Red Cross, the garden clubs, bridge clubs and teas, and luncheons; and I went faithfully to the office in town and read *Barron's* and *Poor's* and the quarterly and annual reports of a thousand companies—truly then, the grim and spectral thought of death did not come to haunt us in our conscious moments. We busied ourselves with our affairs. Sometimes, on the weekends, we opened the house at Adams' Rest and gave parties there and I still went there to shoot in the autumn. We took vacations; in the winters to Delray or Palm Beach, in the summers to Maine or Michigan. In the very depths of the depression, Tavean was born and, two years later, our daughter, Anne.

We did not think of death. And living over again these days in my recollection, I think perhaps we were lured into a false dream of hope by the color of health on Nancy's cheeks, the persistence, indeed the increase of her beauty. It is true that she aged and you could tell it. Nancy's wedding picture stood in a frame in our sitting room and seeing Nancy next to it, I knew that the fleshly face was no longer the face of the photograph. But in its gathering maturity it was more beautiful, the features softened, the smooth white skin as yet unlined. I would look at her and my instinct toward regret at the passing years would be swept away by the sight of her head in full light or silhouette, in fair sun or in soft shaded lamp glow. And her hands slender and smooth, the joints delicately articulated, the fingers tapered. And her legs shining in silk or nylon or when bare, very white, and above the knee, the thighs whiter still and the hips paler than any milk or marble. For me, it was always a great delight to look at Nancy when she had no clothes on—at whatever season or hour of the day, even in the months that preceded the births of our children.

In my youth I had heard stories of men who turned away from their wives when they were with child and for nine months or a year stayed shy of their homes and consorted with loose women or professional prostitutes. But for me, Nancy never lost her beauty, not even when she was pregnant. She was never troubled with morning sickness and in the first months she never grew wan and haggard or sleepy in the afternoon or dyspeptic after dinner. Rather, her face took on a healthy cast, her store of energy was somehow augmented. When her state had begun to show, I would catch her sometimes regarding herself in the mirror as if she rejoiced in the very distortion of her flesh. A pleased, somehow quizzical look would come to her face; she would smile inscrutably at her image in the looking glass.

And for me, too, pregnancy brought a fascination. Often, at night, I would follow Nancy into her dressing room and watch as she disrobed for bed, that I might see her naked and look at the swell in the lower belly and the skin's tautness. Then later, in bed, I would feel for myself the hips and thighs, the firm curve of the stomach itself, and how willingly she would come to me in the darkness!

How willingly she moved across the bed, dragged the burden of her awkward body toward a repetition of the pleasure which had brought her to this state. And I, too—I moved toward her in equally passionate desire, in equal ignorance. For how could I know then how much I would love the coming child or know love's consequence, the cost that might be exacted? After Tavean was born, I used to leave the office early simply to come home and look at him, regard him in his crib or in his play pen on the nursery floor or, later, walking unsteadily by his nurse's side or by his mother's. I know that it is fruitless for a parent to speak of love to one who has never had children, to try to catch the ear of a bachelor or a maid. And I know, too, that it is superfluous for a father to explain to another father, a father's love. And yet, the reality of the love was there, existed then as it always did. I thrilled to the small hand that clung to my finger and to the touch of my lips on the smooth and fragrant cheek.

It was the same with Anne, of course, as it is the same now—I can truly say that I always loved them equally. Yet, when I think of their childhood, I think of Tavean, for it was Tavean who had the first brush with death. This happened in 1940, when Tavean was ten years old and the war had already started in Europe, where Nancy and I had gone on our honeymoon; and in this nation our time of peace was growing short. Tavean resembled his mother. He looked to me, especially when he was young, like a somewhat heavier, stronger, more masculine copy of Nancy, with the same black curling hair, the delicate features—though not so delicate in him—the fine eyebrows, the dark eyes, the grace of movement. He came home from school one afternoon with a heavy cold; two days later he was in the hospital with pneumonia. I recollected from the old time of my youth, how when people got pneumonia they lingered on in a state of great discomfort and high fever until they reached what was called a crisis, a moment of definition in the course of the disease, when the patient either died or made the first big step toward his recovery. But with Tavean it was not this way. The physician prescribed one of the sulfa drugs, which were new in their medical application then, and the worst of Tavean's sickness lasted only a little while. In a few days he was able to leave the hospital.

I remember on the Monday morning after Tavean had been stricken on Friday, the doctor, whose name was Horace Anderson, came and pronounced Tavean much improved. When Horace left the room, I left with him and walked with him to the end of the hospital corridor. He was a short, fat, gray-haired man, devoted to his profession. He smiled a good deal and wore a Phi Beta Kappa key on his old-fashioned watch chain.

"He's in fine shape," Horace said, speaking of Tavean. "At this rate, in a day or two, he'll be ready to go home."

I used some conversational phrase to express my pleasure. We were standing at a window looking over the cold gray courtyard.

Horace was smoking and he puffed thoughtfully for a moment. Then he said, "He's in good shape and next week he will be up and around, almost well. But he has been very sick. A few years ago I could not have saved him."

I said nothing. But I looked, I suppose, panic-stricken, greatly frightened and shocked by the vastness of my fear. Horace peered intently into my face and caught my arm with his hand and shook it gently.

"Not now," he said distinctly. "I am talking about before, when we didn't have the sulfas. Tavean is all right now. He is going to get well now. There is nothing to worry about."

"I know," I said, nodding. "I understand."

But when I thanked him and turned away, I moved like a man not in a dream, but as one dazed, crushed by an unforeseen and overwhelming reality. When Nancy and I had brought Tavean to the hospital, we had both been apprehensive, indeed, even fearful, but the knowledge, the belief that Tavean might possibly die had never penetrated my mind's dull circuits, had never intruded into the chambers of my heart. Now, my legs shook beneath me. I could feel perspiration gathering in small drops on my forehead. I moved up the hall to an empty lounge and sat down there and lighted a cigarette.

Perhaps Nancy wondered where I had gone and came in search of me. At any rate, I remember looking up later to see her standing in the doorway, her head tilted slightly to one side, her expression puzzled, quizzical, and somehow vaguely reminiscent of the way she had regarded herself in the mirror before the births of her children.

"Horatio," she said. "My dear, what's the matter? Did Horace not think Tavean was doing well?"

"Yes," I replied stiffly. "He thinks Tavean has almost recovered. He thinks in a day or two Tavean may go home."

"Then what is it?" Nancy asked again. "What's the trouble?"

And I said, "He might have died. If it weren't for sulfa. If this had come to us ten years ago, we would have lost him."

She said, not lightly, but without fear, with no sense of panic; seriously, but with a tone in her voice more of finality than relief, "Then thank God. Thank God for sulfa drugs and that his sickness is now."

Is this all she could say? Was this all that my disclosure meant to her? I—who should be able to interpret this remark in the light of her subsequent behavior—I, her husband, cannot say. But for me, the man, the father, the physical successor of that earlier physical being who had wept sweet tears at the sight of his grandfather's grave, this was the end of peace if not of promise, the beginning not of wisdom, but of a new kind of fear. *For he might have died.* In the eternity of the long-lived, turning earth, in the generations and centuries that marked the time of man, ten years were as neglible as a mathematical point, fragile as tissue or the heart's frail beat; and yet, a decade had meant the difference between Tavean's end and his survival. And ironically, time that had been my enemy was now my friend. The thought of time's passage which had rent my heart, brought now the sigh of relief to my lips. I slumped in the hospital waiting room chair and looked at Nancy.

"It will never be the same," I said at last.

"What, Horatio?" she asked. "What will never be the same?"

"Him," I replied. Then I said, "No. That's not what I mean. I mean next time they may not have the drug, whatever it is. Next time may be ten years before and not ten years after."

She sat down in the chair next to mine and took my hand.

"My dear," she said, "you must not think these things. He is going to get well now and that is what is important now. We will simply have to have faith and trust the future."

"But he could have died," I said. "Ten years ago, five years ago children did die. Don't you understand? We might have lost him."

"Horatio," she said quietly, "we have all got to die sometime."

"You don't love him," I said viciously. "You talk that way because his life means nothing to you." I said this knowing at that moment that I spoke a falsehood; this is what I said to Nancy, to my shame.

And if, like the wars we read about in history, human lives may have a turning point, this was our Gettysburg, our retreat from Moscow, our Crécy. Or to put it another way, if your days may be summed up in a single image— if one bird singing to a tubercular poet in England can encompass all the beauty that has gone before, symbolize all that which is to come hereafter—this, then, was the image for Nancy and me and for our marriage; the culmination of our past, the seed of our future.

I said to Nancy, *you do not love him,* knowing that she did love him, that this was not true. Meaning when I spoke only that I myself loved him deeply and loved Nancy deeply and deeply loved our daughter, Anne. And that I knew that death lurked in the living blood, the promise of death permeated the living flesh, and that I was not prepared to assume death's stern obligation. Oh, I bridled against the time of loss and thereby hastened loss's day. Thus did I speed the instant of bereavement.

On a night fifteen years later, I stood on the porch of our house in Nashville, the house to which I had taken Nancy as a bride, the house in which during the hours just passed we had celebrated our twenty-seventh wedding anniversary. I waved good night to the last of my guests, went back into the house, and said good night to Anne and Tavean. I remember I found them in the den, laughing and talking about their youthful affairs, Tavean standing with his back to the fire and Anne seated in a leather chair, smoking. So little did I suspect what had happened upstairs, I do not remember much of what I said to them then; so unsuspecting was I that I failed to mark the moment. I remember that as always I took pleasure in looking at them, in being with them, in hearing their voices shape their inconsequential words. And I do recollect too that we spoke of their mother's health. Nancy had been a little ill of late; she had a persistent cough, she was somewhat pale, and a bit less energetic than was usual. The children and I told each other that she seemed to be better. She had enjoyed our party, she had laughed through our anniversary celebration, gaily, at last, had she bade our guests farewell.

We slept in separate rooms now and when I passed Nancy's door, I knocked softly and then called to her in a low voice, but when I got no answer I did not attempt to open the door. I had meant to tell her good night and to tell her that I loved her, but I assumed that she was in bed already, asleep already, and I went to my own chamber and undressed and lay down. Late the next morning, I once more called Nancy. Getting no reply, I tried the door and found it locked. I summoned the butler who forced the latch and we discovered that Nancy had died during the night. She had succumbed, Horace Anderson told me, to an overdose of sedative. It had not been an accident, a lapse into carelessness. It was obvious that Nancy had taken her own life.

But why? She had left no note. I tried to find out from Horace Anderson who had been attending her in the little illness she had just before her suicide. But he would not discuss her case with me until the funeral was over and truly, I do not blame him, such was my grief. Yet, through the day that she lay in state and through the day of her burial which followed, the mystery of why she had killed herself was almost as disquieting to me as the shock of her loss. I had known that she was mortal. From that first afternoon in this house, when I had looked at her after the heat of our passion, watched her lift her champagne glass through a film of tears; from that instant I had known that she might die before me and known for a certainty that we both must die. But I had never dreamed that she would take herself from me, that willingly she would lay violent hands upon herself. Oh, she had done this to me and to my children and I could not fathom the reason. I could not tell why.

At last, when Horace Anderson consented to talk to me it was a little clearer but not less disappointing; nothing he said diminished my anguish or consoled my grief. Her symptoms had indicated a lung involvement. There had been the possibility of cancer, the probability of it even, but only surgery would have made diagnosis sure. Only an operation would have established the truth. There was a chance that she might not have had cancer and a pretty good chance that the cancer might have been operable, that she might have lived.

We were in Horace's office. He sat with his white coat open to show the gold key and the chain across his vest. He was older now, fatter than he had been when he attended Tavean, and the gray hair had grown quite thin.

"Did she have cancer?" I said.

"I don't know," he replied quietly. "There was something. She had a lesion."

"Why didn't you operate then?" I said bitterly. "At least you might have made an effort to save her. You might have tried."

"I was going to," he replied. "Sometime this week. She wanted to wait until after your anniversary."

"But I didn't know," I said. "I didn't know she intended to be operated on. She hadn't even told me."

Horace looked at me and I returned his glance, gazed

back for a stunned moment into his wide and placid face.

Then I said, "And you. You didn't tell me either."

"Horatio," he said, "Nancy asked me specifically not to tell you. I assumed, of course, that she was going to tell you herself."

I did not answer at once and I cannot say now exactly what I felt. The pain of my grief freshened and with this came outrage and anger, and shock once more at this senseless, foolish loss.

"But I loved her," I finally shouted. "Can't you understand that? You respected Nancy. You respected her insane wishes not to tell me of her illness. But why, in God's name, could you not have thought once of me?"

But, of course, he never answered this. He simply repeated that the decision of when to have the operation and whom to tell about it had been Nancy's. She had been his patient and he had done what she asked. He had been willing to abide by the letter of her desire.

That night I broke the news to Anne and Tavean, and I think I wept a little as I talked. I know that my anger was rekindled, and I berated Horace Anderson and cursed him for allowing Nancy to die, and blamed him, in a way at least, for Nancy's suicide. Then I stopped speaking and Tavean rose and went to stand at a window and look out at the night.

With Tavean standing apart from us, it was almost as if Anne and I were alone in the library together. I regarded her in her dark clothes of mourning that made her look older than her years. Or maybe it was not the clothes. Maybe, being almost twenty-four, she had come to her first mysterious feminine maturity and I, parent-like, had not noticed this before, had not seen beyond the recollected image of her childhood. She looked at me with the blue eyes slightly narrowed, the normally full and handsome lips pressed tight together, her full breasts rising ever so slightly as she breathed.

I said, "It was his fault. It was the fault of Horace Anderson. He should have told me."

"No," she said and there was a firmness to her voice, an edge there of stern contradiction. "No. Do not say that, Father. It is not true."

"But it is," I said. "The blame belongs to him and he shall have it!"

"Oh . . . " she cried and rose from her chair.

She stared toward the window.

"Tavean!" she said.

He turned to look at us, turned at the edges of the dim light to gaze at us with those familiar eyes, but the sad cast of his face would tell us nothing.

"Oh," Anne said to me, "you don't know, do you? Oh, even now you don't understand."

And she was right. I did not understand. Not even then.

2
The Recollections of Anne Adams

And I think if it had not been for Tavean I would have told him. I would have said—but what does it matter what I would have said? What is the significance of a word or a paragraph that is never spoken? What I actually did was to rise from my chair, to call Tavean's name loudly, peremptorily; but I had temporarily forgotten how much he resembled Mother. I had neglected to remember that when he turned toward me, he would look at me with Mother's eyes, so that telling Father would be—not like doing it when Mother was watching, but doing it in the very freshness and essence of memory, in defiance of the purely, sharply recollected dead. But more than this. Not only violating the mind's image but going also against the desires of the living Tavean, for his eyes, which were so much like Mother's eyes, said no for him, too.

For that is the way Tavean always was. Father used to say that Tavean was like Mother in more than looks, that he was kind like Mother and gentle against the world. And

I know that for a long time I believed this about Tavean and still believe it, for the story of his life, in so far as I know it, is the testimonial of his gentleness, the evidence of his kindness to all men and things. I say, insofar as I know it, because after I was old enough to begin to understand that a brother might also be a human being and possess some qualities not defined or connoted by the simple term *brother,* he was away at school during the months of fall and spring and winter, and I did not see him very much. But I remember once that the headmaster of Tavean's school told Father that Tavean was a good influence in the dormitory, that he helped to keep the boys from fighting and arguing and the headmaster quoted the passage from the Bible about the peacemakers being blessed and being the children of God. From my own experience, I know that Tavean would never hunt with Father. He would go to the field with Father and he would work the dogs for Father, cast them in the morning and whistle them in at noon. He would take a gun along sometimes—a pistol or a rifle—and use it to test his marksmanship, but he would not kill.

There was, however, more in Tavean's nature than this reluctance to hurt the flesh. His manners went beyond good breeding, they were oriental. He was forever bowing and begging pardon, complimenting and answering softly, not obsequiously, but as if in respect and admiration, so that he succeeded in accomplishing what is almost a youthful impossibility; he was genuinely loved by all generations. He was sought after by his own contemporaries, and pestered by their little brothers and sisters, and smiled upon by doting mothers and old maid aunts. But I am telling this badly, for the spring of kindness ran deep in Tavean. I remember his kindness as a source of mystery to me when I was young.

Once, when I was seven years old, perhaps, and Tavean was nine, Mother and Father were giving a party, and they had allowed Tavean to have a guest for the night—a wiry, redheaded, freckled-faced boy named Harry Buchanan. Harry's own mother and father were downstairs at the grown-up's party and, after the three of us children had finished dinner, we sat in the old nursery that had been made into a playroom and listened with growing curiosity to the sounds from below. We sat as if enchanted by the swell of conversation, the strains of music that came to us softly, distantly up the wide stairwell and down the hall. We decided that when the upstairs servants had retired, we would put on our robes and slippers and creep downstairs and look in at the drawing room or the library. We would go and watch the grown-ups drink their whiskey and I could see the dresses that the women wore.

We did this, but when we had crept down to the foyer, we were frightened by the appearance of one of the caterer's men. We ran not up the stairway but into the back hall and stood in a darkened corner near the door to the den. Through the partly opened doorway—which should have been closed, which certainly Mrs. Buchanan must have thought was closed—we saw Harry Buchanan's mother in the arms of a man who beyond all doubt was not Harry Buchanan's father. I remember in the moment before we ran again, retreated again back into the light and, regardless of the caterer's man this time, back up the stairway, how Mrs. Buchanan's hand moved gently up and down the back of the strange man's neck and how her diamond ring flashed blue and yellow in the lamplight. I remember that her face seemed distorted somehow, seemed to me then to have a look of leanness, almost of hunger, that it did not—in my childish eyes, at least—ordinarily wear. The man's head moved ever so slightly, his lips moved against hers, but they did not draw back. I did not see them end their kiss.

We ran up the stairs in silence and I went directly to my room. So I do not know what Harry Buchanan said to Tavean that night or what Tavean, in his great kindness, said to Harry. But I remember that the next morning Harry went home early, before Mother and Father were out of bed, and Tavean and I had breakfast together in the dining room. It was a beautiful day; late October or early November, with the sky very blue beyond the French doors, and the grass brown and the maple leaves falling. It was, perhaps, a football Saturday, when Mother and Father would go to Dudley Stadium and Tavean would listen on the radio. But we did not talk about football and for a long time we did not speak.

At last I said, "What is Harry going to do?" For it seemed to me that he would have to do something. He had seen his mother kiss a strange man and I thought it his duty to take some action, to do something, though I did not know what.

"He's going to tell," Tavean said softly and an expression of pain came over his face. His mouth tightened. The blue eyes narrowed beneath the wide forehead, the fine black hair.

"Tell who?" I said.

"His father," Tavean said with disgust. "He is a fool and he is going to tell his father."

"He has to tell his father," I said. "It is a matter of honor."

"Honor," Tavean said. Then he said, "It will only hurt his father. It will only hurt all of them. It will only cause pain."

Later in the day, I recollect, I asked Tavean what he would do if he saw our mother kissing a strange man. He replied that Mother would not do such a thing and that I should not speak of it. But I pressed him and finally he said that he would not tell anybody. He would be very sorry, but he would keep his peace.

This did not satisfy me either, did not settle the matter for me any more than our conversation at the breakfast table had. So finally I went to Mother. I told her how we had come downstairs on the night of the party, and what we had seen through the doorway to the den, and what Tavean had said about Harry's causing Mr. and Mrs. Buchanan pain.

For a long time Mother did not speak. She was in her sitting room, on the old love seat that stood before the fireplace. She bit her lip and gazed thoughtfully into the fire.

"Tavean," she said and paused. "My dear, Tavean is like your father. You must try to understand that. They can simply not bear pain. Not their own or anybody else's."

So on that night in the library, after Mother's funeral, I did not tell Father, and I did not know then whether even Tavean understood. He peered at me reproachfully from the shadows and I turned away at last and went up to my room.

    The days and weeks that followed Mother's funeral, the time of acceptance and readjustment was difficult for all of us, and you would think no harder for Father and Tavean than for me. They, at least, had their work in the city. They would go in to the office on Union Street and do whatever it was they always did, divert themselves reading the Translux, I suppose, or listening to the old men who came in to watch the quote board. You would have thought that this would be enough and that, for an interval of time after Mother's death, they would have been content to come home at night and read the paper and look at television and go to bed.

But it was not this way. For one thing, they began to drink heavily. As soon as they arrived from town, they would go straight to the den, straight to the bar, and out of some perversity, shame perhaps at what they were doing, they would not even let William, the butler, attend them. They would mix their own highballs and gulp them down, and sit with glasses in their hands staring at each other. Then, after dinner, they would have liqueur or brandy and pace the floor and stare out the darkened windows and argue sometimes about stocks or about football or basketball. But they did not lose their tempers and often a long silence would fall and I would see them look covertly at one another. Tavean would gaze at Father with his lips slightly parted, an expression almost of bewilderment on his face. And Father, who did not look grief-stricken in spite of the tears that he occasionally shed,

Father would turn his even profile toward Tavean, the light glinting on the gray in his hair, and his brown eyes would open wide in a kind of wonder.

Except that they were drinking too much, Father and Tavean behaved themselves rather well. But whatever I said, whatever I did, I could not find a way to stop their drinking. They would get up early on Sunday morning and go with me early to Holy Communion, and then with the Communion wine fresh in their stomachs, they would return home and have a toddy before breakfast. They would drink before luncheon on Saturday when they were home and I suspected they drank at noon during the week downtown, but concerning this, of course, I had no way of knowing. They began to have long discussions on the relative merits of different brands of whiskey. Tavean drank Scotch and Father drank bourbon. Father would ask Tavean why he thought Haig and Haig was better than Dewar's, or he would discourse on the difference between Jack Daniels and Old Crow. Finally, in an effort to stop them and because in their company I was very, very lonely —because I was lonely through the day with nothing to do, no office to go to, no reports to read, and lonely when they came home and sequestered themselves in their whiskey—I allowed Philip Holcomb to come at night and call.

Philip was a tall man with broad shoulders and horn-rimmed glasses who taught history at Vanderbilt. I had known him when I had been a senior at Vanderbilt and we had had coffee together sometimes, or sometimes in the afternoon gone off campus to drink beer. I had dated him many times since, and he had been in our house attending the party on the night that Mother died. Now I allowed him to come and visit, sit for a few hours at night with me and with Tavean and Father.

But even this did not help. Or rather, it did help, but not in the right way, not in the fashion that I had anticipated. I would not let Philip come until eight-thirty or nine at night and I made it a point that he see Tavean and Father, if only for a little while. In the beginning, I hoped that Father and Tavean would at least stay sober until Philip got to our house and then they would not have so much time to get drunk before they went to bed.

But they did not stop drinking. They went on taking liquor before and after dinner just as always since Mother's death, and when Philip came they insisted that he drink with them. They were too far gone, too gay, when Philip got there to have sense enough after they greeted him to go upstairs or to another room and leave us alone. They would start in on him with their idiotic talk of whiskey.

Father would say that by all means Mr. Holcomb would have to try some of this very special Very Old Fitzgerald. Tavean would say he begged Father's pardon, but that Phil was a man who could appreciate Ballantine's; or, if Tavean were in what he called one of his periods of deviation, he would offer Philip some Old Overholt or some Tullamore Dew. And Philip, being a man I suppose, or maybe just being Philip, would have a drink. He would say, "Yes, thank you, sir," and when I was seated, he would sit down himself; and now there were three of them sousing up liquor, instead of the two I had had on my hands to begin with.

Oh, I do not really blame Philip. He is no more to be

blamed, I suppose, than any human is to be blamed, being human and therefore subject to the heritage of man, to the sin of Adam and Eve and to the flesh's weakness. He realized that I was fond of him and that I wanted to see him. But he was aware too, I think, that I needed his help. He knew that I was concerned about Father and Tavean, sensed this somehow, as a man will sense things, and then resumed the masculine habit of blunt stupidity. He knew that I wanted him to cheer up Father and Tavean and so, being Philip Holcomb, Ph.D., a man with much knowledge and a cynical air, innocent gray eyes, and an innocent, youthful smile, he could think of no possible way better to cheer up other men than to sit down with them in the den and help them pour the whiskey.

And at least, the conversation noticeably improved. There was still some talk of football and of Getty Oil and U. S. Steel. But we managed to get away from White Horse and Old Taylor and get on to the Civil War—which was Philip's specialty—and on to Confederate generals and the old Army of Tennessee and the Battle of Van Buren which was of great interest to Father. I remember those evenings by the plethora of names and dates, times of attack and the directions that the armies took, and the maps that Philip would draw—sometimes from memory. The air of the den was full of names and for Father, and for Tavean too, I think, the old names rang thrillingly like the sound of bugles. Johnson and Hood and Hardee and Polk, Bragg and Cheatham and Cleburne and Forrest; Perryville and Murfreesboro, Chickamauga and Atlanta, Brices Cross Roads and Fort Pillow and always, at last, the grand and wonderful Confederate defeat at the Battle of Van Buren.

One night, Philip asked Father why Great-grandfather Adams had not been buried at Adams' Rest, why if he had been killed so close to home, he had not been interred in his own family graveyard?

"I don't know," Father said. "My Aunt Irene didn't know. We are not even sure who buried him. None of the family was living at Adams' Rest. My grandmother was dead by then. The children were with Grandfather's sister in Nashville."

Father paused. Then he said, "The slaves were gone, too. They had all run away. Can you imagine that?"

Philip smiled and said yes, he could imagine it.

Then Philip asked Father whose corps Grandfather's brigade had been a part of. Father told him General Stephen Lee's, and Philip looked puzzled. He opened his mouth as if he meant to speak. Indeed, he did make a noise that might have been the word *but,* or might have been only a grunt, for the sound stopped abruptly. Then he took a sip from his glass and nodded his head without looking at Father and said: "It was a good corps."

Later, I walked to the door with Philip to tell him good night. I let him kiss me. I even returned his kiss—not the way I wanted to, but demurely as befitted a girl in mourning. Then I drew back and took a deep breath and asked him what it was that he had almost said to Father.

"When?" he asked.

But there was no use for him to feign ignorance. He looked at me sharply, his eyes narrowed a little, and I knew that he remembered and he must have known that I knew.

"It was not much of anything," he said finally. "It was just that I think maybe Horatio was mistaken about General Adams' corps. At Van Buren, Lee's Corps didn't get to the field until the shooting was over."

I was surprised.

"But it was Lee's Corps," I said. "I know that. Father has checked the records. He has even looked at the old muster rolls in the State Library."

"Yes," Philip said. "I guess we needn't worry about it."

He told me good night and moved out onto the porch. Then he turned back and spoke to me out of the shadows. "Don't mention that about Lee's Corps to Horatio. There are all sorts of reasons why General Adams might have been at Van Buren early. We know where corps and divisions were during the different engagements. But who can say about the individual officers and men?"

"I won't," I replied.

And, of course, I didn't. I didn't tell Father what Philip had said about Great-grandfather Adams' corps.

Father and Tavean continued their drinking and Philip continued his visits through the rest of the fall and through the winter, but in the spring—for some reason that was then unknown to me—the drinking stopped. Back in February, I had suggested rather testily to Father and Tavean that they might think of giving up liquor for Lent and, in keeping with the natures that they both exhibited during this period, they very courteously promised to think over my suggestion. Indeed, on Ash Wednesday they kept the fast and sat with smudged foreheads through a dry cocktail hour. But on the day following, they returned to their bottles, took up their drinking again, as if Our Lord had never suffered on the cross or risen from the dead on Easter morning. I think I lost patience with them then. I gave up. I ceased to try to make them stop drinking. And, of course, it was at this moment, apparently, that they chose to reform.

I know that after the beginning of Lent, I left them to their own devices. I kept a good deal to my own suite upstairs and I went out occasionally with Philip—to late movies sometimes, or to his apartment to dinner, or motoring, or riding in the park. I still saw Tavean and Father at mealtimes, in the morning and at night. I was courteous to them, solicitous even of their happiness and health, but for a while I refused to sit with them in the afternoon when they got home from town. Then maybe I noticed some alteration—some change in Tavean's evening demeanor, or in Father's, some slight improvement in the quality of their speech. Or maybe it was simply intuition or, more than likely, it was just plain feminine curiosity, but one afternoon I returned to the den.

And they were not drinking. That is, they had one drink, or maybe Tavean had two. Then they put their glasses aside and went sober to the dining room and later had no brandy, no liqueur. The first night I did not trust what I had witnessed. I suspected Tavean and Father of some sort of pretense, some subterfuge to make me believe what was not true. But the next night it was the same and the same again the next night, and then they ceased to make a point of coming to the den in the afternoon at all.

Tavean began to play golf and often he would eat at the country club, or he would simply go out to have dinner with some of his friends. Then Father began to play a little golf, too, and he found reasons to remain in town sometimes beyond his regular working hours. Suddenly it was over, the period of foolish intemperance was ended, the drinking had stopped.

The cessation had come strangely. Both Father and Tavean had come to their senses at apparently the same time, but at whose design or behest or instigation? Had Father first stopped drinking and thereby given Tavean an impulse toward sobriety? Or had Tavean stopped first and in his new rectitude been a reproach to Father? Had they simply grown tired of drinking, burnt out their taste for whiskey, or had they agreed beforehand on a day that their debauch should end? For a while there was no way for me to tell, no way of knowing.

But I remember looking at them and thinking to myself, who has at last decreed this end to mourning?

Now, of course, I know that it was neither of them. It was Emily. It was Emily who had caused them to rise up again to assail the world. Once, a long time after this, Father tried to explain to me how it had been, how he had come first to notice Emily and first to love her. We sat in a hospital waiting room, and I suppose Father had to talk, had to say something against the hospital silence, against the minutes that passed so slowly, and against his fear. And I suppose, too, that he had to try to explain it to himself, show himself why it was his fate to be here now, waiting here on the couch next to me.

At any rate, he said, "Did I ever tell you how I met Emily?"

"No, sir," I replied.

Then he said, "No, not how I met her. That is not how it began." He paused. "It was one afternoon downtown," he said. "I got on the elevator and she was already on, already standing over in one corner. I thought at first only how young she looked and how very beautiful and, for some reason, I wanted to hear her talk. That's silly, isn't it? I mean, I know what the psychologists say, I know about Freud. But it's funny that whatever motive, desire, I had would manifest itself in just that way. I thought if once I could have a conversation with her, hear her speak, hear the tone of her voice, and what she talked about, then —but I don't know what then. I hadn't planned ahead. I just wanted to hear her." Another pause. Then he said, "That's one of the first things I noticed about your mother, the way she talked, and with Emily it was the same way. It's almost like history . . ."

He broke off with a look of great pain on his face. Then the doctors were in the room walking rapidly toward us.

So I do not know the rest of Father's story. I cannot say when it was that he first heard the sound of Emily's voice or where he was when he heard it or what they talked about. I myself saw her first on a summer night when Father brought her home to dinner.

I knew about her before this, of course. Tavean had seen her and it had been Tavean who had told me that Father was going out with her, that he was not working nights after all as I had innocently suspected. Philip Holcomb had met Emily, too. He had come across her and Father in a bar downtown and he had sat at their table for five minutes or so and talked to them. But neither Philip nor Tavean could tell me much about her. Both being men, they had not seen much beyond the almost silver blond of her hair, the shape of her legs, the way she smiled when anyone spoke to her. And she was young. Tavean told me that she was about his age; that she could not be much over twenty-five or twenty-six.

Even so, I suppose I should have been prepared for Emily. I suppose I should have known even then that what a man thinks of as feminine beauty is a far cry from what you see in the fashion magazines, does not even resemble those skinny models with their sucked in cheeks. I should have known that in spite of what Father told me later, it would not matter much whether she could talk or not or if she talked, what she said or what language she said it in. She did not need to know how to talk. She needed sense enough only to know when to cross her legs and when to lean forward slightly toward Tavean or Father.

I know that when I first saw Emily she was very frightened, scared I suppose at the size of Father's house and afraid of the servants and of Tavean and of me. She stood with Father at the door of the library, her lips held rigidly in a half smile, the cheek muscles taut beneath the powder. Looking back now, I blame myself sometimes for that moment. I had nothing against her, nothing to forgive her for, except that my own father had found her attractive. And Father had invited her to our house; whoever she was and wherever she had come from, she was our guest. It was my place and duty to rise with more alacrity than I did rise, to smile with more warmth, to move more rapidly toward the doorway to receive her hand. I think sometimes that with a little courtesy—or maybe courtesy is not the word, perhaps the word is love—with a show of welcome and affection I might have made us all happier in the days that were to come.

But what I did, I did, and that was to get up slowly and look at her for a moment before I spoke. Oh, it was not obvious. I did not stare and clamp my lips together. I am certain that neither Tavean nor Father noticed any hesitancy on my part, any reluctance in my behavior. But Emily saw, Emily knew, and while I looked her over she stood stiffly in the doorway, her face with its half smile immobile, or more than this, hard and frozen, like the mask of comedy, like a face of stone.

I looked at her and I saw what the men would have called her beauty. Her hair was silvery blond, as I have said, cut short and brushed back and whoever had cut the hair and dyed it for her had done his job well. The blond hair glowed softly, dully in the light and below it the face was round, the brown eyes big, the mouth full, and the nose small, almost delicate. She was a tall girl; standing there now in heels and a short, black dinner dress, she was fully as tall as Father and I would have been tempted to call her fat, though perhaps that would be less than accurate. For she was well-proportioned. Considering her size, her over-all dimensions, her hips were no wider, or not much wider than they should have been. And I do not mean that she was a giant, an amazon. Father was five feet, ten inches tall and with her shoes on, Emily stood as tall but not taller than he. She just seemed big, there seemed always to be a great deal of her. And I remember that her long and tapered calves always gave me the impression of nakedness somehow, even when Emily was wearing stockings. And maybe that was it. Maybe that is what men look for. Maybe that day in the elevator when Father first saw Emily, it was her legs that he was looking at, after all.

On that night when Father first brought Emily home to dinner, the conversation, even with Philip Holcomb present, was as strained and as meaningless as you would have expected and the end of the evening was a moment of relief. Yet later, when Father had told Tavean and me that he meant to remarry, I made a sincere effort to become friends with Emily and she, I believe, tried to make herself fond of me. I met her in town a few times for luncheon, a quick snack eaten in a cafeteria that we might have time later for shopping or a walk in the sunlight around Memorial Square. For Emily was still working. She was the secretary to an insurance agent and through the week she had only an hour off for lunch. I felt a little sorry for her then. She was so awfully pressed for time, which would not have mattered so very much if she had not been equally pressed, or even worse off, for money.

She was shopping the good stores and she had obviously been in them before. There were clerks in them who knew her name and the clerks were nice to her. But it was apparent from the beginning that Emily did not dare make a mistake. A hundred dollars or even fifty spent for the wrong thing would put her trousseau out of balance; she had no margin for error, no reserve. One day I bought her a present. She was looking at dresses and I wandered over to the perfume bar and simply on impulse—or maybe out of a long held, subconscious pity for her struggle with money—I got a bottle of something, a Chanel number or Joy, perhaps, and had it gift wrapped and gave it to her.

I handed her the package at the entrance to her office building and she stood for a moment with a stunned look on her face, her eyes opened wide and filled with wonder. She did not say anything, not even thank you, and at last it occurred to me that she thought I was giving her a wedding present; and because I was Father's daughter, because of some suddenly discovered delicacy in her nature, she was embarrassed by what she must have considered a gesture on my part. But a gesture of what? What was it about a gift from me that she did not trust?

Obtuse as I am, caught up as I was then in my own thoughts and plans and sorrows, it took me a while to find the answer; a few days passed before I understood. On the afternoon that I gave Emily the perfume, she did say thank you finally, but in the insincere manner of a child who has had to be reminded. She turned and fled into her building and I did not see her again for almost a week; then, when we met, it was by accident. I was driving through town and I saw her standing on a corner. Apparently, she was waiting for a bus.

But when I stopped and spoke to her, she did not seem to want to admit that she was waiting for a bus or even to admit that she was standing on the corner while, on every side, people walked past her and behind me horns began to blow. For a moment, it was almost like being back in college, back in philosophy class with the ghost of Bishop

Berkeley, and Emily was an ideal projection of my own consciousness. But beyond the surface ineptness of this little image was the fact that no ideal entity would behave so erratically as Emily was then behaving, or evade so falteringly the questions that I asked. Where was she going? She did not say, she merely mumbled. She had not had lunch, she was not going directly back to the office; she seemed almost panic-stricken, and I do not believe she would have got in the car with me if a policeman had not come. I was blocking traffic and I think Emily leaped into the front seat beside me in an effort to save me from arrest.

As things turned out, I have always regretted that I stopped that day and held up traffic until I had made Emily get into the car. For what I saw then, what I found out about Emily, was none of my business really. I had no right to pry, no right to know. She was on her way home. She lived with her mother and Mrs. Hopkins had locked herself out of their house. Only Emily had another key.

It took me a long time to find this out from Emily. She did not want me to take her anywhere, she did not want to tell me where she was going; but she was in my car and I kept on driving and all the time that we were riding around the city, Mrs. Hopkins was waiting on her own front porch.

Except there was no front porch and not much house either, walls and a roof and these tight enough, I suppose, with the fat, drab-looking woman seated on the doorstep. It was not a slum. I must be very careful to make that point clear, just as I must try not to make myself sound more snobbish than I really felt that day in the car with

Emily. It was a little frame house in a neighborhood of little frame houses. The street in front was rough with the pavement cracking. The alleys were narrow and the lawns were ragged and here and there a few bright flowers grew.

I went in with Emily. Oh yes, I did that. It takes a lot of maturity, a lot of wisdom to know how to let go, to back off from the foolishly contrived act, or to extricate yourself from the consequences of your own good intentions. So I did not say, "I will wait for you in the car." When she said, "Won't you come in?" I went in with her.

And what is there to tell of that visit, except that Emily did not look like her mother, or did not look much like her, though perhaps in her youth, Mrs. Hopkins had had her own type of beauty, too? The house inside was clean, too clean, too much uncluttered for the smallness of the rooms. There was a television set and a couch and a few chairs. There was a rug on the floor of the living room and there was a congoleum rug on the floor of the dining room, and through an open door, I could see the edge of a rose bedspread which was draped neatly over a hollywood bed.

Mrs. Hopkins offered to fix us our lunch. I declined and Mrs. Hopkins then offered us a glass of iced tea and we declined this also. I think Mrs. Hopkins was going to say something to me about Father, about what a fine man he was, perhaps, or how much she admired him, but I am not sure of this.

She stood for a moment looking rather thoughtful; a portly, wrinkled, middle-aged woman with rough hands, flat-heeled shoes, no stockings, and a gingham house dress and perhaps Emily could tell what she was thinking. For when Mrs. Hopkins opened her mouth, Emily spoke quickly.

"We have to go," she said. "I have to be back at the office."

As an afterthought, she glanced down at her watch.

Emily and I moved out the door, out into the brilliant summer sunlight, moved toward my car that glistened brilliantly in the sun. And then I made the third mistake of the afternoon. The first one had been making Emily get into my automobile, and the second one had been going in to meet Mrs. Hopkins, and the third one was the effort I made now to deny what I had just done and seen.

I have learned since then that it is not always best to gloss things over. I had been with her to her home and it would have been better for me to let her know some way that I took into account the fact that she was poor, and that I was rich, and that Father was rich, and that she was going to marry him. Somehow, I should have admitted all, I should have exposed the entwined circumstances of our lives to our joint scrutiny. But how do this, by what fine speech or pregnant gesture? What I did was to smile weakly and she tried to smile weakly back.

I said, "Why don't you take the afternoon off? Why don't we go shopping or go have a drink somewhere?"

"I can't," she said.

I started the car and we rode in silence for a while.

Then she said, "I love Horatio. I do. I love him." She made this declaration as if to the world, but only I was there; only I heard it.

She told of her love in a quivering voice and, looking back, I wonder why I brought her so much pain, why I treated her the way I did that day. For, certainly, I had no cause to wish her evil.

Father and Emily were married in Mississippi on a Saturday in September, less than a year after Mother's death. Or at least, one hot Saturday afternoon Father came downstairs with his suitcase and said good-by to Tavean and me rather sheepishly and got in his car and drove away. I remember, when Father had left, I sat in the library with Tavean, silent, wondering how long it would take Father to drive to Emily's, and how long it would take them to drive to the town where they were to be married, and whether they would actually be married today or tomorrow. I thought, ironically, that if the ceremony were to take place around midnight, they might not actually know. They might be uncertain for the rest of their lives when to toast their anniversary. And thinking of anniversaries, I thought of Mother, who had gone upstairs and killed herself on hers.

I glanced at Tavean who was seated across from me and the eyes that were so much like Mother's looked a little sad.

"Well," I said, "are you going to start drinking again?"

"Ah, little Anne," he said, brightening, "did we bother you with our drinking?"

"No," I said, "I loved it. But this time I think I'll join you. If you start again, I think I'll come to the party too."

The smile of levity left his face. He crossed the room and knelt by my chair and put his arm around me.

"Little Anne, little Anne," he said gently, "I know you hated what we did. I know you were lonely. But don't you see? You are stronger than Father. He needed me more."

3
The Life and Times of Horatio Adams

On a hot afternoon in September, we drove south through middle Tennessee, past the brown stubs of the harvested tobacco fields, south into the cotton country and, at last, across the state line into Mississippi. Late at night we stopped in a small town where, in the basement of the courthouse, the marriage license clerk was always on duty and we got our license and were married by a justice of the peace. I remember how we left our car parked in what by daylight would be the shadow of the Confederate monument, the stone soldier, who represented a flesh and blood soldier who had fought in the same army with my Grandfather Adams and we walked beneath maples along a quiet pavement to the frame house half a block away where a porch light burned.

Was I nervous at this, my second marriage? More so, I suspect, than I was aware of then, although I recollect that my limbs seemed to tremble ever so slightly and that, when I spoke to Emily, my voice had a strange quality, a catch as if I suffered from some shortness of breath.

Emily was very beautiful. During the long afternoon's journey, we had kept the car windows closed and the air conditioning unit on, so when we got to the little courthouse, no hair of her head was out of place, no perspiration stained the small of her back or the silk of her collar.

However, she refreshed herself before the wedding. At the house of the justice of the peace who, in spite of the light left on above his door, had been sleeping, she went off into the back of the house with the J.P.'s wife, who would be our witness. I remained in the living room, standing uncomfortably before the mantel which had been decorated with some artificial flowers and some candles—tapers, I think they are called—and a small, very plain Protestant cross that was in need of polish.

I had not expected to see an improvised altar and I had not counted on being married by a man so young, for in the movies and in the occasional newspaper pictures you see, the justice of the peace is an old and hoary man, with his nightshirt not quite completely contained by the waistband of his trousers. But this man, our justice, had taken the trouble to put on his shirt. He was not over thirty-three or -four years old and he had great locks of thick black hair and a sun-tanned face and a college fraternity ring on his finger.

And I suppose he was surprised at us, too, after all his experience of marrying seventeen-year-old girls and nineteen-year-old boys who claimed, on the papers they signed at the courthouse, to be at least eighteen and twenty-one, which are the respective ages of legal accountability or consent or just reason, perhaps, in Mississippi. But however this was, however miscast we all were for the roles we filled, we stood up by the mantel and had our ceremony.

It was a ceremony that was unfamiliar to me. It was, I suppose, what is called a civil ceremony and it differed in many respects from the service in the *Book of Common Prayer,* by which, so many years ago, Nancy and I had been married. But why not, when all else was so different too? I know that all my life, I had remembered the afternoon of my wedding in Cleveland by the faint smell of old incense that had permeated the old church, the pure reds and greens and blues of the sunlit windows, the embroidered white silk of the priest's vestments. Now, there was only the smell of the Mississippi house, which was no smell really, the absence of any smell at all, as if the air itself were artificial, like the flowers. And there was the bare cross with no figure, no memento of passion; and here, in the living room, a few chairs and a worn carpet.

But there was Emily in a sheath dress of very thin, brown, dimly figured silk, and brown silk shoes, and stockings that caught the light when she moved in front of me. For soon, very soon, we did move—out the door and into the night again and back up the street to the automobile and the stone monument. In the car, I kissed her but, of course, not for the first time, and kissed her this time no differently from the other times, feeling myself not quite married, not quite yet beyond the stage of courtship. Then I drew back and she said, "Darling, I love you," and I kissed her once more.

But then, where were we to spend the first night of our honeymoon? Beyond the little town in which we were married, there were several tourist courts. They looked very much alike, rows of shingle or frame or sometimes masonry construction, with the offices all glass and brightness out in front and neon signs showing vacancy or no vacancy; but on this night, most of the courts had room. As much as I loved Emily, as much as I wanted her at that moment, it did not seem to me that any of these tourist courts would do. They seemed too obviously designed for our situation, for what we intended and, it seemed to me, that our entry into one of them would somehow be too flagrant. So we rode on through the Mississippi night toward the resort hotel on the Gulf where we had reservations.

Emily slept part of the way. There was a bottle of cognac in the glove compartment of the car and once we were well out on the highway, on the long straight road through the flat country that goes on forever without turning, I opened the cognac and we had a drink and smoked while the cognac burned in our mouths and then drank again and smoked again and were mostly silent. Emily sat very close beside me and I let my hand fall on her leg and rest there and then I moved my hand a little and felt the thin silk brush against the very thin, taut nylon of her stocking. Then with my hand still outside her dress I moved my hand upward and felt the cloth very smooth and slick against her skin and the little round knob of the supporter catch and above this the bottom edge of her girdle. And I know that this is what a million men have felt, moving their hands along a million legs of a million different shapes and ages and descriptions. And I knew then that when I lifted the dress to feel the stocking and the cool flesh itself, I would be doing once more what men had always done, what my forebears and the forebears of all men had done back to the time of Cain, at least, if not of Adam. And I did not do it.

I let my hand rest on Emily's leg for a moment more. Then I removed it and had another drink and drove on down the straight road, listening to the motor and the beat of my heart, watching the long white line that had no turning. I did not explore her person further because, perhaps, of the same sense of dignity and appropriateness which, in the first place, had kept me from stopping at one of the tourist courts. Or perhaps I held back out of a feeling for my own individuation, my separateness in the flow of the world's time. Or perhaps even then I was delaying against the moment of pleasure and marriage's consummation. For what is consummation except a commencement? And every beginning discloses—if only in its incipiency—the inevitable end.

With Emily's head on my shoulder, her eyes closed, her legs, in sleep, just slightly parted, and her dress pulled just slightly up above her knee, I drove and watched the sun rise in Mississippi. Outside now it was cool. I turned off the air conditioning and opened the window and I could smell the Gulf in the damp coolness of the morning and, beyond the road, the black earth had changed to sand. When we got to the hotel, the night clerk was still on duty.

Riding up in the elevator with the bellboy, Emily leaned against me. She was not quite out of her sleep and her body felt very warm against mine and very much relaxed, so that her hand rested on my arm more heavily than it had ever rested before and it was strange being with her so early in the morning; for always before I had seen her in full daylight or at the cocktail hour or in the evening. The old desire which I felt for her, and which had never left me, which had resided with me all through our courtship, though at some times it had been stronger than at others, came to me very sharply now. I shifted my position that I might feel again in its freshness, the initial touch of her person, the weight of her flesh.

We went into our suite, a sitting room with a balcony that overlooked the Gulf, a bedroom with long windows, a dressing room for Emily, a bath for me. I ordered breakfast and left her alone for a few moments while I shaved quickly and took a shower. When I came back out wearing my robe and pajamas, she had hung up my clothes in a closet with her own. I wanted a cigarette and I could not find my coat. Then I opened the door to her closet and there was the dress she had worn in our wedding, the silk wrinkled slightly from the long ride, and her slip and my suit beside it, and on the floor the brown silk shoes. I was touched by this evidence of her thoughtfulness and excited by this view of our clothes hanging together. I got my cigarettes, and I frankly snooped, opened drawers in the bureau until I came to her brassiere and her girdle, these wrinkled too from the long ride, and the stockings which had been stretched wide by the fullness of thigh above her knees. For a moment, I had to wait and smoke and breathe deeply, look out through the window at the green, easy tide, that I might gain control over my own flesh and enter into Emily's presence in decent order.

The breakfast had come and she was drinking coffee. She was seated in a chair with a summer robe pulled around her, a long, lace-trimmed, silk negligee, not quite white and not quite translucent, but it settled loosely, flowingly over her figure, to show the turn of her crossed leg, the curve of her hips, the flatness of her stomach. She too had been to the shower and she wore no makeup. Around the edges of her face, her hair was wet. I knew that now there need be no more waiting. That we did not have to eat breakfast or delay for the sake of propriety or hold off against the conventional hour for going to bed. I knew that I had only to kiss her and to catch her hand and lift her gently up and walk with her with my arm around her waist into the bedroom. And I did kiss her and caress her and feel the curves of her body beneath the silk of the negligee, which is a feeling of released flesh that is very intimate and very tempting, and in a way better, sometimes, than the feel of the naked skin. Once more my desire made its physical preparation, but we did have breakfast. I did not lift her up.

I sat and looked at her and wanted her, and the steam from our coffee rose in the air between us. The sunlight came in strong at the windows and glinted on the silver dish covers and brightened the pale beige carpet at our feet. I do not know what Emily thought of me at that moment. I do not think that she had expected me to delay while we ate our eggs and our ham and our biscuits. It must have occurred to her, as it did to me, that for the rest of our lives there would be meals to eat, breakfasts and luncheons and dinners no less savory and nourishing than this. And indeed, it was the thought of the time to come, the quick running sands of our future life, that held me back. In a moment or five or ten, we would go to our bedroom. She would remove the negligee under which she wore nothing and I would see—as in my fevered imagination, my distraught mind's eye, I could almost see now—those last inches of flesh which I had never seen, the secret planes and articulations of pale stomach and smooth hips and the secret hair, darker than the hair of her head, which the beauticians attended. This, in my fancy, could I almost see.

This and the moment that would follow it, I delayed against.

Because when the desire is very strong, when you are caught up in the simple, aching want, you are like Joshua and the sun stands still; or in your passion you think the sun stands still, which is to you, in your hiatus of deception, the same thing. There was only Emily and the world did not exist; and not existing, the world did not spin or orbit and there was therefore no night or day, no winter coming. There was only the round face, the hair ends slightly damp, the full figure covered in silk, the silk-covered buttons tight over the breasts, the hand poised holding the coffee cup, and on the other hand the engagement ring and the wedding ring which I had placed there.

Oh, I would keep this moment, that we might not plunge into our days. That for a small, small while, we might retain our love secure, immune in the confluent universe from the conjunctions of the stars, unbroken by the sharp cry of love and by love's quick motion.

But, of course, it was not by love that the spell was

broken but by love's climax, the drawing back from the poets' little death to life's measured seconds.

Or, at least, that is the way I thought of it later as I lay beside Emily just before I went to sleep.

During the days of our honeymoon, we would spend the mornings at the beach playing in the water, walking on the sand, and at noon, we would come back to the hotel and have a drink and put on our clothes and go down to luncheon. Then after luncheon sometimes, we would go back up to our rooms and go to bed sometimes or maybe just read or talk or listen to a baseball game on the radio. On other afternoons, we would get the car and drive out along the Gulf, out to the rough stretches where there was no beach or where the beach was narrow and very steep and we would watch the birds above the foam and the slow-moving ships against the skyline. At night, we would go to a bar sometimes or to an amusement park where I won a little china dog for Emily by knocking down a stack of bottles with a ball. But in the evening, wherever we went, we would come home early and undress early and, once or twice, I was able again to achieve that fine and wonderful desire that shut out all suggestion of the rest of the world and left us suspended in time together.

We were growing very brown from our daily exposure to the sun and our muscles were in tone from the daily exercise of swimming. At night, after we had made love, we slept very well and always in the morning, I woke before Emily. I remember that I would lie very still for as long as I could and then I would move carefully and touch Emily very carefully, put my hand on her hip or thigh, and not stroke her, but just let my hand rest there. If she were sleeping soundly and it did not appear that she would awake for a long time, I would get up and dress and go out and read the paper in our sitting room. I would rise softly and close the door softly behind me and the sitting room seemed always very bright to me when I had just come from the dim bedroom where the blinds were drawn. The weather remained fine every day of our honeymoon and every morning in the sitting room, the sun came strong through the long windows, just as it had that first morning when I had sat at breakfast with Emily and wanted her so much. Now, with Emily still asleep in the bedroom, I would order coffee and smoke and watch the gray-blue smoke spiral up through the yellow sunlight and watch, beyond the windows and down below, the stretch of white sand and the waves moving up on the white beach, reaching up as gently as the touch of love.

The bellboy—a tall, middle-aged Negro—had learned to knock softly, so when he came, he did not wake Emily, and he did not speak when he came into the room. He simply smiled, broadly, a little secretively, as if there were something wonderful and mysterious in the fact that Emily was still sleeping. It was the smile that people smile over a baby's crib, but not quite; it was richer, it contained something more. When the bellboy had gone, I would look at the headlines and look at the market quotations, and the sports pages and editorials sometimes. But I did not really give a damn whether Jersey Standard was up or down or whether the Braves were going to win the pennant or whether the columnists thought the world was coming to an end. I cared only for the beauty of the day and for the sight of Emily and the sound of her voice. My attention was always diverted a little, divided by my listening for the first sound that she would make.

Then, at last, I would hear it. Maybe the noise of her footsteps, but more often the sound of water, the toilet being flushed or the shower turned on: I would know she was awake and moving in the world and soon the door would open and I would see her. I liked being in the brightness of our sitting room, knowing that she was awake in the room beyond. I took pleasure in having her coffee ready for her and the chair waiting where she would sit and have breakfast with me. Then, she would be there and for us, the day would start.

Sometimes, in the afternoons, we would lie on the beach and plan what we would do when we returned to Nashville. I would ask her if she wanted to go to the football games and she would say yes, and that part would be settled. Then we would talk about parties that we might go to after the games, and we would talk of concerts and dinner dances at the country club and winter vacations and where we would take them and the steeplechase in May. Then it would be summer and time for another vacation, and then September and we would have been married for a year.

Twelve months would then have passed and she would be twenty-seven, still coming into the fullness of beauty, maturing as really handsome women do mature and I—I would be fifty-seven and the thought was painful. The naming, to myself, of the number, the counting of my years, would catch me up suddenly in the midst of my happy dream and I would fall silent and gaze off at the sky. I remember that in my first marriage, I was fearful of what time would do to Nancy. Now, being not only older, but wiser, I was very much afraid of what time must do to me.

"Darling," Emily would say, "what are you thinking?"

I would put my hand on hers and say, "Of you, my dear. I always think of you."

In early October, with the weather still warm and the world still green from a recent rain, we ended our Mississippi honeymoon and returned to Nashville. We went to the house where I had taken Nancy, but not to the same suite; we used the rooms that I had used alone during the last years of my first marriage. And I think Emily was very fond of our house, for on the afternoon that we got back from Mississippi, we went over it together and she exclaimed again and again over its size and the beauty of its appointments, the arrangement of the rooms and the grounds and the garden. And for a while, at least, I think Emily was very happy to be my wife and to live in my house with me and Anne and Tavean.

At first she seemed a little shy. She spent a good deal of time in her own sitting room; often, I would find her there when I came home from work. She did not have much to say at dinner, particularly when both Anne and Tavean were present or when Anne's young man, Philip Holcomb, was our guest. She was careful about a lot of little things. No matter what the rest of us did, she would never have more than one drink before dinner, and she seemed reluctant to take the first bite at the table and reluctant to ring for the servants at the end of a course.

We entered slowly into the social life of the city. At first she wanted to go to the club only on off nights during the week when there was no special entertainment and most of the members would be likely to dine at home. Many times, on Friday or Saturday or Sunday night, we did not even go out but rose from the table to make our way upstairs to watch television or read or sit by the fire, sit with our chairs pulled close together, or sit together on a couch, very close to each other. But this was all right with me, too, for friends will keep or you can find new ones and the country club will still be there, and next week or next year, there would be more parties just as good as the ones we were missing now. There would be time again for the sound of music, the clink of ice in the full glass, the table covered with canapes, the talk progressing as the night progressed, swelling in the mellowness of the moment. Time sufficient for this there would be; but now in my vessels, the blood ran fresh and Emily sat beside me in a plainly cut, jersey dress and medium-heeled, kid slippers, her legs extended toward the hearth, and my arm was around her shoulder. Or, Emily stood beside the mantelpiece in a dull green tweed skirt and a white Oxford cloth shirt, fastened at the collar with a golden pin and the cuffs held together with golden cuff links. Or, in our sitting room, Emily rested on a stool with her knees drawn up and her arms around her legs, and the dress was the black silk that she had worn to church and she wore black suede shoes and dark stockings. Oh, she was beautiful beyond compare and I was content to be alone with her beauty.

* * *

Perhaps, admiring her, loving Emily as I did, I did not try hard enough to make her feel at home, to help her fit into this new world in which she found herself. There were things, of course, that Emily would never be able to do. For example, she would never be a member of the Junior League, as Anne was and as all Anne's friends were, but I did not know then whether this made any difference to Emily. In the weeks that followed our return from Mississippi, Anne and Emily often went to lunch together and often they would meet some of Anne's friends, and I believe that almost everyone was nice to Emily. Emily, however, was at a disadvantage, because the ladies that she met now had college connections and were members of sororities and the women's talk would often come around to the old days at Wellesley or Vassar or Duke or Vanderbilt or to the Tri Deltas or the Thetas or the Pi Phis, and then Emily could do no more than keep her silence. What I say now, of course, is only my own conjecture, but I can imagine that often a new acquaintance would turn to Emily and ask where she had been to school. And how would Emily answer this? Name the public high school she had been graduated from or mumble that she had not been to school, had attended no college? I do not know, but I believe that she must have suffered through some distressing moments.

And it will not do to say, what does it matter? To say that Emily should have been accepted for what she was—a bright, good girl who was very pretty. For in the world that Anne introduced her to, Emily was a stranger. She did not know all the old gossip, all the old ramifications of family, the ancient glories and remembered scandals which were the folklore of the country club, what the novelists call the enveloping action of Emily's and Anne's daily lives. If Emily had been born somewhere else, no matter where, if only sufficiently far from Nashville, all would have been different. Her ignorance of the Nashville past would have been accepted and patiently, gleefully rectified, but being from Nashville and not knowing, Emily was suspect.

At least, this is the way I look at it, the way I think things must have happened, looking back. But to return to the ground of my certain knowledge; toward the end of October, Anne announced one evening that she was going down to spend a few days at Adams' Rest. On the spur of the moment, it seemed a good idea for all of us to go. The weather was beautiful, the days bright and the mornings cool, the afternoons perfect for riding on horseback, the nights made for sitting in front of a fire. Emily had never seen Adams' Rest. I wanted to take her there and show her the house, and to go with her over the Civil War battlefield and to show her my grandfather's grave in the Confederate cemetery. Tavean, too, was agreeable to the trip.

We went down to Adams' Rest on Tuesday, the thirty-first of October, Anne and Emily making the trip in the morning, and Tavean and I driving down in the afternoon when our work was done. And I must confess that during the trip from Nashville to Van Buren, it did not occur to me that this day was All Saints' Eve and that Anne had most likely gone to Adams' Rest to pray for her mother. I know that when I got to the house, Emily was waiting on the front porch and I kissed her, and then we went in and crossed the hall and walked up the stairs together and into the room where Nancy and I used to stay. It was a long bedroom at the back of the house. At one end, near the windows, there was an old tester bed, made of walnut and furnished with a green silk canopy. Then there was a walnut press and a large washstand which served as a dressing table, and, at the other end of the room near the fireplace, there were a love seat and a pair of upholstered rosewood chairs. This room was as I had always remembered it. Except for the net curtains and the cloth of the bed's canopy, nothing had changed since I had come here to hunt with Uncle Billy and I suspected that very little had altered since the day when my Grandfather Adams rode away to war.

I turned to Emily and kissed her. Then I stood back and held both her hands and looked at her; I examined the round, smooth face, the full lips that were very red, the clear brown eyes, the graceful neck, and the tight fit of her shirt and her riding breeches. In the room at the old house at Adams' Rest, with the day fading, the light beyond the windows growing dim, I looked at my wife and was glad that she was young. My heart celebrated her youth and her youthful beauty.

Then there was a knock at the door. I released Emily's hands, took out my handkerchief and wiped by lips, then hurried across to the door and opened it.

Anne was standing in the hallway. She was apparently fresh from her dressing room. The bracket lamps in the hall were on and, by their glow, I could see that her makeup was freshly but lightly put on, her hair was newly combed and she wore a plain black dress, black shoes, and, except for her watch and a small ring, she wore no jewelry.

"I am going to Van Buren," she said. "I wanted to tell you."

I didn't understand at first. "All right," I said. "We will wait for you. We will hold back dinner."

"No," she said, "that doesn't matter."

But she did not leave. She stood looking up at me in silence, her face white beneath its thin coat of powder, her hair and her eyebrows very dark.

So finally I said, "Is Tavean going with you?"

And she said, "No. I expect Tavean will make his own arrangements. I did not ask him."

Then, of course, I understood.

"Wait a minute," I said. "I must tell Emily." But tell her what? How explain it to her? I did not try.

I took a step back into the bedroom, started to shut the door and hesitated, unwilling to close the door while Anne stood before it. But Anne, herself, reached in and took the knob and pulled the door gently to. Emily was sitting on one of the rosewood chairs near the fireplace. There was an expression of bewilderment on her face. Her eyes were narrowed, her lips were slightly parted, and sitting there in all her youth, in all the fullness of her youthful flesh, she waited for me to move across the floor and speak to her.

"My dear," I said, "I am going to Van Buren for a little while with Anne."

"Now?" she asked.

"Yes," I replied. "Now. I must."

We reached the little town in first darkness, and around the square, the pavement was beginning to fill up with spooks. Boys and girls of all ages were abroad in costume—witches and clowns and pirates, rabbits and dogs and indiscriminate characters with horrid, horrid faces and flowing sheets. We drove past them slowly and they blew their horns at us, rattled their noisemakers, and shouted, "Trick or treat." But we did not stop until Anne got to the church.

It was a very old church, one of the oldest Episcopal churches in Tennessee, and it was very small, and, at this time of day, dimly lighted. There were a few rows of pews with an aisle between them and then the altar rail and the altar itself, with the crucifix flanked by candelabra. And to one side, back from the altar, but near the front, there were rows of votive candles in red glass holders. I stepped inside the door with Anne and then paused, stood back in uncertainty, looking at the crucifix and the red, flickering reflection of the burning candles and at the worn carpet and the old cushions of the altar rail.

But Anne did not hesitate. She moved down to the front of the church, bowed, and moved into one of the pews, knelt, and crossed herself, and remained for a while motionless. Then she arose and bowed again to the altar and went to the side of the church and lighted one of the candles and bowed again and returned to her pew, crossed herself again, and resumed her prayers. I sat down in the back of the church.

I knew that she was praying for her mother, saying some office for the repose of her mother's soul, but I, not being as High Church as Anne, did not know what. I did not know whether now she would use her Rosary, or whether there was a form of prayer which she would repeat, or whether she would make up the prayers herself as she went along. But I knew that all this really did not matter.

What mattered was what I was going to do. And I knew that some Episcopalians, some priests I had talked to, did not believe at all in purgatory and believed but little in praying for the dead and others, at the other extreme, would say that there was no use praying for Nancy's soul for she was not in purgatory but in hell because she had committed suicide. And maybe what mattered was not, after all, what I was going to do but what I myself believed in. And I found that I could not answer this question. Or perhaps I could have if I had really wanted to. Maybe I could have if I tried.

What I did was to sit in the little church where Anne would come to Holy Communion tomorrow and wait, while Anne's candle burned and while Anne prayed. Being near the door as I was, I could hear the sounds from off the street; the horns and the noisemakers, the shouts of the children, heard dimly and from afar and, in their quality, more gay than ghostly. I wondered where Nancy was and I wondered if she were anywhere, and I wondered what it would be like to be really sure one way or the other. It seemed to me that if you could really be sure that there was a heaven and a hell after death, then you could live like the priests said you ought to live without any trouble. And if you could be absolutely certain the other way, that death was an end and nothing else—but this, of course, was one of the things that had bothered Hamlet. Strangely, I thought of this; I, who had seen no ghost come up from the grave. I, who was called upon to wreak no vengeance.

So in the end I did not pray. Finally, Anne crossed herself for the last time there in the church and bowed to the altar for the last time and I held the door open for her and we moved out onto the sidewalk. She was crying, not audibly, but there were tears on her cheeks. She took out her handkerchief and wiped her eyes and blew her nose gently. Then we both looked up to see the children standing near our car.

I did not know for sure whether they were boys or girls for they looked at us from behind their hideous masquerade faces. One was a gypsy and another was an Indian, and in between these two was a very small child, perhaps four, not over five years old, dressed in the suit of a skeleton, the mask of a skull. The little skeleton held to the gypsy's hand, while Anne went through her purse and found some chewing gum to give them and then we got in our car and returned to Adams' Rest.

I drove and, when we were out of town, I put my hand on Anne's and patted it and said, "Darling, darling, you must not sorrow so."

"I'm all right," she said in a voice that was a little flat. "I'm all right, now. Don't worry."

When we got to the house, Tavean and Emily were having cocktails. There was a pitcher of martinis on the table by the fireplace and Tavean's eyes were growing a bit red, and even Emily had had more, I think, than she customarily took.

Tavean gave us an expansive welcome. He poured drinks for Anne and me, and he chided us for being late and for depriving him and Emily of our company. Then he said gaily, flippantly, "But I am not really angry. I have had a good time just sitting here talking to my stepmother."

Actually, there was nothing wrong with what he said, for the word he used told only the truth, but it fell on our ears more sharply than the vilest obscenity. Emily blushed and stared at the floor. I do not know how I looked, of course, but Tavean himself blushed, and I think that his referring to Emily as his stepmother was almost an accident, so quickly had the thought struck him and so immediately—thoughtlessly after his martinis—had he spoken.

Anne's face only got whiter. She said, "For God's sake, Tavean, try to use some taste."

In strained silence we went into dinner and in silence did we sit down at the table. I remember that I gazed about me, looked about at my wife and children, regarded their faces by the flickering candlelight.

4

The Recollections of Anne Adams

I REMEMBER our trip to Adams' Rest as the beginning of a bad time, though what happened that week was, perhaps, only the initial climax, the first fruition of pain which had long been making. However this was, for at least some of what happened I must blame myself. In the first place, I should have known, after my experience with Father, to leave well enough—or bad enough—alone. On All Saints' Eve, I had made Father go to church with me and he had sat in the back of the church while I prayed for Mother, not praying himself, or at least not appearing to, and I had succeeded only in subjecting him to suffering. I had made him think of what he did not want to remember or consider and at the end, I had let him see me cry.

This should have been enough. But the next morning, I awakened Tavean and made him go to church, too, made him take Holy Communion because it was All Saints' Day; and because I got him up early, he decided to go on to the office in Nashville, though the night before he had planned to remain at Adams' Rest. A few miles out on the highway, he topped a hill going very fast and came up suddenly behind a truck loaded with tobacco. He had his choice of ramming the back of the truck or ramming head-on into the car coming toward him or leaving the road. It was like Tavean to take to the field. He slammed on his brakes and pulled hard to the right, jumped the gully and knocked down a section of fence, hit the pasture and slid, skidded for a hundred feet or so on the slick wet grass. Then the car turned over and slid for a good distance more with Tavean rattling around inside and holding on, I suppose, to the steering wheel, until at last the car came to rest on its side with the top against an elm tree.

This cost the insurance company, I don't know what, for a new Thunderbird for Tavean. But more important, Tavean was hurt and he was hurt worse, I think, than he and the doctor who attended him ever admitted to Father and Emily and me. When the accident happened, the tobacco truck and the other car, the one that was heading toward Van Buren, both stopped. The two men in the truck got to the accident first, but the door which was up was locked and they could not get it open. They could see Tavean lying against the other door, unconscious, limp, his knees thrown up almost against his chest, his left foot turned at an odd angle, his ankle or his leg obviously broken. This did not frighten the two farmers as much as the fact that one of Tavean's hands had fallen across his face, and somewhere beneath this hand, Tavean was bleeding badly. The blood was making a puddle on the cream-colored upholstering of the door.

The man from the car which was going toward Van Buren was halfway across the pasture when the men from the truck called to him that they could not get the door open and it seemed to them that Tavean was in danger of bleeding to death. I believe, perhaps, they thought he was dead already, for the bleeding was beginning to slow down now, but they instructed the man in the car to call Van Buren for help. He returned to his car and drove till he reached a house. A few minutes later, an ambulance came for Tavean.

Besides the broken ankle, Tavean had suffered a bad gash on his forehead. This had accounted for all the blood, of course, but the bleeding had stopped by the time the ambulance got to the wreck, and the car door was pried open so the attendants could get him out. He suffered a concussion and there were possible internal injuries, though I do not know even yet how serious these were.

When Father and Emily and I got to the clinic where Tavean had been taken, it was still early in the morning and we did not know any of the details of Tavean's accident. The nurse, or whoever it was who had called Father, had told him only that Tavean had been injured. Now in our anxiety, we almost ran up the walk and we moved quickly through the glass door into the reception room. We were fearful already and the clinic reception room with its chairs and potted plants, its vague hospital smell, its quietness, would have been enough in itself to compound our fear.

But already present in the reception room were Mr. McMurtry, the police chief, and Mr. Rutherford, the editor of the Van Buren newspaper. They were talking in hushed tones to the girl at the desk. Considering the size of the town, the infrequency of crimes or accidents, the scarcity of news, Mr. Rutherford and Mr. McMurtry would most likely have been there if Tavean had done no more than scratch his elbow. But as rational as this explanation of their presence was, in the intensity of the moment it did not occur to me. Seeing the two men and the girl talking softly, I thought Tavean was dead, and Father and Emily must have thought him dead, too, to judge by the looks of surprised pain that etched their features. I remember that the color drained from Father's face. He was a handsome man, his flesh lined but not sagging, his eyes bright and vigorous, his chin strong. Now, suddenly, in the space of a second or two, he was overtaken by age. The new gray of his complexion disclosed pouches above his cheekbones, his lips were thin and bloodless, as old men's lips are thin. There were minute beads of perspiration on his neck.

Emily grew pale, too. She turned to Father and saw no help for her there. She turned toward me and called my name, and then she sank down slowly onto a couch and started crying. I recollect that she put her hands over her face to hide her tears. At the sound of her weeping, the girl at the desk hurried across the room to reassure us.

"Now, now," the girl said, putting her arm around Emily's shoulder. "He is going to be all right. The doctor is with him now and he is going to be fine. You mustn't worry."

Tavean did not regain consciousness on the day of his accident. Or rather, after the X-ray pictures had been taken and the cast had been put on his leg, he roused himself and began to talk, but what he said did not make any sense and when he tried to get out of bed, the doctor put him under sedation. When Father and Emily and I saw him, he was resting quietly, breathing deeply, his ankle and his head both grandly bandaged.

I stood by his bed for a while and felt sorry for him. Then I knew he was going to be all right and I got angry thinking what a fool he had always been. I remembered all the times he had frightened me, going down the highway with the speedometer needle pushing a hundred or bouncing over country roads, flying up and down steep hills as if the car Father had given him for his birthday were a roller coaster. I wished I could wake him up and say, *I told you so,* because, God knows, I had. I had told him to stop driving the way he did and I had begged him to stop it and I had threatened to tell Father about it, but nothing had helped. He had always looked at me and smiled and said, "Little Anne, what's the use in having a car if you can't make it hop?" And another time he had said, "That's living, little Anne. You've go to keep moving fast to be sure you're still alive."

Now, looking down at him, I said, "Fool!"

Emily stared at me in astonishment.

"You never rode with him," I said. "He drives like a maniac. I doubt if even this will teach him a lesson."

On the way home from the clinic, Emily began to cry again. It was late in the morning now, almost noon. The day was very beautiful; the sun bright, the air clear, and on each side of the highway, the fields sloped away, rolled gently toward the easy hills and the autumn sky. In the pastures there were beef cattle grazing. Father was driving and Emily was in front with him and I was on the back seat of the car smoking. I was still a little angry at Tavean, but mostly I was indulging myself in that sweet weariness that comes when the danger is past and the worry is over. Emily turned to look out the window, moved so I could see her face in profile. There were tears glittering on her cheek, spoiling her makeup. After a moment, she turned back to look at the road and Father glanced at her and he, too, saw that she was weeping.

"My dear, my dear," he said softly. "Everything is all right now. You don't have to fret any more. Tavean is going to recover."

"I know," she replied. "I'm sorry. I just can't help it."

But Tavean's accident was not the only thing that happened to us on the first of November. As you would expect in a Southern town, there is a statue of a Confederate soldier on the square in Van Buren, and for a Halloween prank, somebody had painted the statue green. It was not a pretty green such as you see on house shutters or the dull, olive green you would expect a soldier to be painted. Our Confederate soldier was a bright, yellowish, nauseous green from the bottom of his boots to the very tip of his bayonet. His hands and face and clothes were green, and with green eyes he stared north in search of Yankees. I had seen the painted monument on the way to church and I had known that Father would be annoyed about it. But I had not known then that the vandals had been in the Confederate cemetery, too. In the graveyard, angels and crosses had been painted the same hideous color and the marble shaft above Great-grandfather Adams' bones was green.

Father did not hear about the painted monuments until the afternoon of the day of Tavean's accident. The clinic to which Tavean had been taken was on the south side of Van Buren, so Father had not driven past the square and the statue and, under the circumstances, it had not occurred to me to tell him what had happened. After leaving Tavean's bedside, we drove home and had luncheon. Then Father and Emily professed to be tired. They went upstairs to take a nap and I sat down in the living room with a magazine.

I was in a Queen Anne chair by one of the front windows, thumbing through *Vogue* and looking at the pictures, when I heard an automobile on the drive. It was the Van Buren police car, coming to a stop now in front of the house and for the second time that day, fear gripped my heart. For a moment, I thought again of Tavean, but there was nothing ominous or hurried in the way the car came to a leisurely stop or in the manner in which Mr. McMurtry got out from behind the steering wheel and ambled toward the door. He moved slowly, like a man in the grip of some thorough but slight confusion. He was about Father's age and he took great pride in the fact that he had served thirty years in the army and retired as a master sergeant after the Korean war. His police uniform was always neatly pressed and when you drove past him on the street, he was likely to salute you. Now, coming up onto our porch, he carried himself very erectly, but there was an unmilitary and very quizzical smile on his long, tanned face. I hurried to let him in that he might not ring the bell and disturb Father and Emily. He had come to tell Father that the monument in the cemetery had been painted green.

I went to awaken Father. I went up the stairs and knocked, and I suppose he and Emily were not sleeping, for Father answered immediately. I told him that it was nothing concerning Tavean, but that Mr. McMurtry would like to see him downstairs.

Later, in the living room, Mr. McMurtry stood almost at attention and said, "Mr. Adams, they have painted the soldier on the square."

"Who?" Father said. "Painted what soldier?"

"That Confederate boy," Mr. McMurtry replied. "That stone statue. They have painted him all over as green as grass."

Father tilted his head slightly and his forehead wrinkled in an expression of surprise. "Painted the Confederate soldier?" he repeated, his voice soft and incredulous.

"Yes, sir," Mr. McMurtry replied, "an ugly green."

"But why would anybody want to do a thing like that?" Father asked.

"Last night was Halloween," I said.

And Mr. McMurtry said, "Yes, sir. I expect some boys done it for a prank."

Father moved close to the chair where I had been sitting and stood looking out the window. He spoke with his face turned away from us. "I don't understand it," he said. "I don't know what the world is coming to. I don't know what people are thinking of, anymore."

He paused, and then he did turn and look at us. "Why, when we were boys, Mr. McMurtry, we played jokes, of course. We unhinged gates and soaped windows. But we would no more have thought of desecrating that monument than we would have . . . " He stopped talking, not able, apparently, to complete the comparison, to find the proper image.

"No, sir," Mr. McMurtry said, "we surely wouldn't."

"I hope you catch them," Father said, his voice edged with anger. "This has gone beyond boyish mischief. This is vandalism, Halloween or no Halloween and it's got to be stopped."

"Yes, sir," Mr. McMurtry replied. Then he straightened his shoulders a little more, stood a little more like a soldier at attention, and told Father the rest of what had happened—which was the worst. "That's not all," he said. "Them boys, whoever it was, went to the Confederate cemetery, too. They painted a lot of the headstones out there. They painted your grandfather's."

"They what?" Father said. "Well, damn their times, they've got to be caught. I'll offer a reward. I'll pay to see them captured."

For a moment we were all silent.

Then Mr. McMurtry said, "What do you think I ought to do, Mr. Adams? I mean about getting things cleaned up. The mayor's out of town and I don't know who to ask to do anything."

"I don't either," Father said. "I think I'd better go to the cemetery and look at the marker."

I went with them. Father and I got our coats from the hall closet and we got in Mr. McMurtry's yellow police car and drove toward town. After we were on the highway, it occurred to me that nobody had told Emily where we were going, but I suppose Father had simply failed to remember her. His mind was too much occupied with the Halloween vandalism.

We rode in silence, Father and Mr. McMurtry in the front seat and I in the back. Like a prisoner, I thought. Like the loose woman being taken down to headquarters by two members of the vice squad. The thought struck me as funny and I chuckled out loud. Father turned in his seat and frowned at me, scowled like the teacher used to scowl sometimes when I was in grammar school.

Then we were in town and the Confederate soldier was green, all right. He was just as green as Mr. McMurtry had said he was, except hearing about him from Mr. McMurtry was not like seeing him. He was enameled. He glittered greenly in the autumn sunlight and there was a crowd of teen-agers milling noisily around the pedestal. There were boys in denim trousers and flannel shirts and girls in skirts and sweaters. Just as we started our slow turn around the square, a blond boy about twelve or fourteen years old climbed up on the pedestal and leaned with his head propped on his hand, his elbow resting on the statue's green thigh and the boy closed his eyes as if he had gone to sleep there.

"Look at that," Father said. "Look at that, Mr. McMurtry."

Then Father stuck his head out of the car window and shouted, "Get down from there! Get off that monument, you little roughneck!"

For a moment, the children were silenced by the tone of authority in Father's voice and the markings of authority on the police car. Then the boy on the statue held his nose as if he were going to jump into deep water; at the edge of the pedestal he flexed his knees, made a great leap and shouted, "Splash," when he landed. The other boys and girls gave a loud cheer. By this time, we were around the square and driving away.

"Idiots!" Father said.

"It is because it is painted," Mr. McMurtry said, explaining. "They never climbed on that statue much when it was just stone."

At the cemetery, we turned off the highway and followed the little road that ran for a while between the gravestones; that divided, circled, and came back in an easy curve to the marble shaft of my great-grandfather's grave. Looking over the field at the crosses and angels, the chiseled slabs, the vases of withered and not so withered flowers, the faded and not so faded miniature Confederate flags, it occurred to me that whoever had been running wild with a paint brush had at least learned a lesson in history. The Civil War had been a big war and the Battle of Van Buren had been a big battle—here a long time ago a lot of men had died.

I guess in a way it was a lesson for me, too. In a way, I was like the children in town who had never thought to climb on the monument until somebody painted it. In my time, I had been here often with my father. Times beyond counting I had visited these graves. I remembered a dozen Confederate memorial days when the May sun was bright on the Confederate colors, bright on the stones and the new-mown grass of the graveyard, and bright on the graying hair of the old ladies who read poems by Henry

Timrod and Father Ryan. And I remembered other, less public visits, in winter with the sky dark and the ground wet from rainfall, and in summer with the maples in full foliage, and in autumn—as it was autumn now—with the leaves turned but not yet fallen, the trees red and yellow above the dead brown earth. But never before had the graves seemed so many. Never before had I stopped to calculate the loss.

Now, I was surprised by how few stones the vandals had been able to cover. And yet, at least a hundred of the largest markers were painted green.

We stopped at Great-grandfather Adams' monument. We got out of the car and stood and looked. Under the paint, the inscription was still legible, and familiar as it was to me, I read it over; I think Father and Mr. McMurtry read it, too, for they did not speak.

>Sacred to the Memory
>of
>Tavean Van Buren Adams
>Brigadier General, CSA
>Born Adams' Rest
>Van Buren, Tennessee
>April 22, 1822
>Killed in Battle
>near the town of Van Buren
>November 27, 1864
>Gentleman, Scholar, Patriot
>He kept the faith

We stood and read, and I know that this moment must have been a time of poignant sorrow for Father, because he loved this grave in the same desperate, fearful way that he loved everything else that was dear to his heart. But he gave no sign of sadness. No sigh escaped his lips. No tear came to his eye. He simply continued to stand, his face pale and drawn, his mouth tight, his brow not furrowed but the lines there more distinct. At last, he reached slowly into his pocket and took out a small penknife and opened it and went to the stone and began to scrape gently at the paint.

"Mr. Adams," Mr. McMurtry said, "a painter will know how to get that off. He can use some kind of remover. He won't have to scrape it."

Father continued to cut at the paint until a little white patch of marble was showing. Then he closed the knife and put it away.

"Yes, sir," he replied courteously. "I'll have it taken care of. We won't wait for the mayor. We won't wait for the town council with all their red tape."

We remained for a while longer in the cemetery. Then once more we got into the police car and we went back home.

Around noon on Friday, two days after his accident, Tavean was brought by ambulance to Adams' Rest. The doctor had not wanted to release Tavean. I believe they had quite an argument before Tavean left the clinic, the doctor insisting that Tavean remain where he was for another week or so and Tavean declaring his intention to go to our house in Nashville regardless of what the doctor might advise. They ended by compromising on Tavean's coming to Adams' Rest, which was, I think, what Tavean really wanted. I believe now that he mentioned Nashville in the first place only that he might appear partially to heed the doctor's counsel and seem to give in—a little bit, at least—to the doctor's will.

However this was, he did come to Adams' Rest. He was installed in the large downstairs bedroom which must originally have been intended as the master bedroom but which, according to family legend, no one had ever permanently occupied. We had always kept it as a kind of guest room. It was behind the library, below the room that Father and Emily slept in; and it was twenty-five feet long and twelve or fifteen feet wide, with a cherry bed and chest and dressing table at one end and parlor pieces, living room furniture at the other. There was a molding around the ceiling and the mantelpiece was marble. There were two long windows that looked out over the side lawn and other windows from which you could see the stables and, beyond the stables, the fields, and back toward the house, more lawn, and off to the left, the fence of the family graveyard. But for a while at least, Tavean had to enjoy the view from his bed. And the rest of us had to stay at Adams' Rest to help him enjoy it. Indeed, Tavean was very easily bored, and Father and Emily and I spent most of our days and nights in his room punching his pillows and lighting his cigarettes and sharpening our wits to keep him cheerful.

He lay in bed in pale blue pajamas, or in gray pajamas with a fine white stripe, or in yellow pajamas neatly figured with little men playing golf, and for part of the morning, he was content to read—the newspaper, magazines, novels. But he always grew tired of reading before noon and during the day there was nothing that he wanted to see on television. So one of us had to be available to talk to him. Even when he was watching the television set, he liked to have somebody nearby that he might complain about the plots of the dramas or share the joys of seeing a well-executed right cross. He required our company as long as he was confined to his room at Adams' Rest.

The time that followed Tavean's accident comes back to me in a thousand fragments, moments remembered in isolation of what was then a smooth succession of many days. There was a gloomy morning with a fire burning in the fireplace and a lamp burning on a table and Emily and me seated at the foot of Tavean's bed. It was soon after Tavean had come from the clinic and, as a result of his concussion, he had not regained his depth perception completely. He reached for a glass and misjudged its position and spilled the water on the table and on himself. Emily, quicker than I was, rose and wiped the water off the table. She squeezed the few drops that had fallen on the counterpane and the few spots on Tavean's pajama cuff. Almost as an afterthought, almost unconsciously, she kept on with her drying and wiped Tavean's hand.

And one afternoon, just at dusk, I entered the downstairs bedroom and there was no light this time except the flame of a cigarette lighter poised in the air between Tavean and Emily. I remember seeing the two faces in half-darkness, half-silhouette, the two heads and the flame composing a motionless tableau. I could see Emily's smooth profile and the edges of her silver hair, and Tavean's somewhat pale face and his lips smiling. Then

Tavean leaned forward and puffed and the lighter was extinguished.

And one day at noon, a bright day, the kind of day that comes in Tennessee in November, when the air is warm and it is almost summer again, I was in the room and Emily entered wearing brown flannel Bermuda shorts and long, brown, ribbed socks and a pongee shirt and brown loafers. I think I came as near that day as I ever came to understanding what Father had seen, what his reaction had been when he had caught his first glimpse of Emily. What I saw now was something that a man could perhaps visualize when Emily wore a street dress and stood back against the drab decor of the elevator car. Somehow, it seemed that clothes were altered, modified by Emily's touch or by the mere accident of coming into her possession. The pale tan color of the pongee shirt was heightened by the dull silver of Emily's hair, and the cloth seemed thinner against her skin; by some trick of the bright, midday sun, I could see through the silk the narrow white brassiere strap. But there was more than this. The shirt was not tight, but the material clung to her flesh. It nestled over the curves of her breasts, it lay flat and unwrinkled against the flatness of her stomach. And below the neatly pressed shorts, above the neatly folded socks, the large, smooth, white knees were a naked confirmation of the tan shirt's promise. She was in her way quite beautiful. But what I saw now had nothing to do, really, with what I had always thought of as beauty when I looked at other women, other girls. For a while, I did not dare turn my gaze toward Tavean.

"Hello," Emily said. "Good morning, Anne. Good morning, Tavean."

"Good morning," I said.

And Tavean said breathlessly, "Yes. Oh, yes. Good morning, Emily."

This is the way things went during the days of Tavean's recovery, but at night it was different, with Father back from the office in Nashville seriously discussing business with Tavean. They would talk about bond issues and the fluctuations of the market, and it appeared to me that neither of them was interested in the conversation but that each of them kept up his end of the talk out of consideration for the other. It was in a way like the nights they had spent with each other just after Mother died, each of them drinking—as I now believe—to keep the other company, for both Tavean and Father were very polite and they loved each other. Then, after the talk of business, Father would return to the subject of the painted monuments, which remained for the Van Buren police departmen an unsolved crime.

I remember that on a Saturday night a week or so following Tavean's release from the clinic, Philip Holcomb drove down from Nashville to have dinner with us, and he saw the green soldier on the square. There had been some trouble in finding a workman to clean the statue. Father wanted, as he put it, "a man experienced at removing paint from statuary" and since, I suppose, most statues don't get painted, Father was having trouble locating a man he was willing to trust. So Philip got to see the Confederate soldier colored green.

He told Father that he rode around the square twice, admiring the green accoutrements and the jealous complexion of the soldier's face. Father did not seem to think the joke was funny. We were in Tavean's room—where else did we congregate in those days?—and Philip was standing near the fireplace, his drink beside him on the mantel. He looked very tall in a gray tweed jacket and dark gray trousers. Smiling at Father, peering at Father through his spectacles, he looked not quite scholarly, not quite cynical.

"That uniform marks him as one of Sam Hood's men," Philip said. "Marse Robert wouldn't have tolerated such an awful shade."

Father smiled tightly, mirthlessly and said without humor. "Yes, I see. I suppose not."

"Aw, come on, Horatio," Philip said, his voice kind, but still a little bantering, "I know it makes you mad. But the boys around here have to do something. You don't have a symphony orchestra for them to listen to. Or a city museum."

Emily giggled. "That's right," she said. "That's what we've been trying to tell him. Tavean and I."

"Yes," Father replied testily. "That's what you've been trying to tell me. Except you and Tavean make it sound even more like a joke."

We were all embarrassed by Father's obvious annoyance, by the look, almost of anger, on his face. For a while no one spoke. Tavean and Emily glanced at each other and Tavean kept on looking at Emily, but she let her gaze drop away. Philip took a sip from his drink, set it down, and then picked it up immediately and took another sip. Father rose from his chair and took a step or two toward the door.

"I'm sorry, Horatio," Philip said. "I didn't mean to be rude to you. I don't really think painting monuments is the best way to spend an evening."

Father stopped. "I know," he said and he was speaking more quietly now. "You're all just too young, I guess. You just don't understand it."

He paused. Then he said with more asperity, "But when I was young, I understood. I've been revering my grandfather's memory, going and paying my respects to his grave ever since I can remember. And there never was a time— even when I was a little boy—when this business would have struck me as the least bit funny. I don't know what's got into people these days. And you, Philip. You're a historian. You ought to know that if we lose our sense of the past, we lose our identity in the present. Isn't that true? Each generation doesn't just start all over. We're what we are because of the past. And what we are will affect the future." Father waited for Philip to answer.

Philip said, "Yes, I know. It may not be that simple, but that's part of the truth, at least."

"It is the truth," Father replied. "And Tavean is an Adams. I ought not to have to say these things to him. And Emily."

His voice softened when he spoke Emily's name. He looked at her fondly and moved across the room to stand beside her. He rested his hand on the back of her chair. "And Emily," he said, the soft voice almost pleading. "My dear, you too are an Adams now. Maybe, since we haven't been married very long, you forget that sometimes."

"No," she said, sitting rigidly straight. "Oh, no. I don't

forget. I never forget that I'm married to you. I always remember."

There was a moment of silence. Then we moved into the dining room and when dinner was over, Philip and I went to a movie.

We drove in to Van Buren and went to the little theater and ate popcorn through the first reel and watched the bright colors and the pretty people. But I could not get my mind on the story. I kept thinking about Father and Tavean and about Emily in her Bermuda shorts and about the statue on the square that someone had painted. I remembered how I had come to Adams' Rest in the first place because I had wanted to pray in the church here and light a candle on All Saints' Eve for Mother. The rest of them had come because I had come, and now Tavean lay with his ankle in a cast and his head aching and his eyes not focusing right—though focusing right enough to see Emily. And Emily was giving him something to see; her face in the magic shadows of the lighter flame, the shape of her breasts beneath the thin silk of a pongee shirt. Father was fretting over a Halloween prank, and all these things seemed somehow to be connected. It was easy enough to see that Tavean's ankle would not be broken now if he had not come to Adams' Rest and he would not have come to Adams' Rest if I had not come to pray for Mother. You could go back beyond this, of course, and say that I would not be here if Mother had not died, and Mother might not have died—but no matter about this, for if you once catch hold of the past, there is no letting go this side of Noah. Returning to the present, I knew the connection between Tavean's accident and my prayers, but there seemed also to be other connections that I could not establish. Somehow, Tavean's injury seemed to be related to Father's wrath at the green monuments, and related to both was Emily and her fine beauty and her flat stomach and her naked white knees. Maybe, I thought as the movie played, it was just that all things seem to be connected once they have happened. Maybe, indeed, I was just jealous of Emily, being myself not so very tall and weighing a little more than I would like to weigh. Maybe, but I did not think so.

Later, back in the parlor at Adams' Rest, I sat on the love seat with my head on Philip's shoulder and we talked and smoked and watched the burning fire. I had offered him a drink which he had refused and I was very glad that he had refused, for I did not feel like drinking. It seemed to me sometimes that all we did at Adams' Rest was to sit and look at each other and guzzle whiskey. Maybe that was all right when Philip wasn't with us. Maybe then, things being the way they were, we all needed bracing. But Philip was here now and I was in love with him, and one of the symptoms of love is that even the simple, idiotic things are enough to make you happy. Through the last reel of the movie, he had held my hand and I had enjoyed sitting there like a country girl, having my hand held in the little country picture house. I had felt like the queen of all the world and I still felt that way. As I sat there in cold sobriety with Philip, the spell was still on me, and I found that I could even think of Emily and Tavean and Father without being much disturbed.

I looked at Philip, let my eyes range over the soft ivory-colored shirt, the black, knit tie, the dark, curly hair, the dark-rimmed spectacles, the nose a bit too long, the smile that could never be quite convincingly cynical. It occurred to me that Philip and I were different from the rest of them—from Tavean and Emily and Father. They were as handsome as the gods; Philip and I bore the marks of man's mortality. But more important than this was what I did not understand then. Those other three knew something that Philip and I could not dream of. Philip Holcomb, Ph.D., and Anne Adams, B.A., were babes in the woods compared to those three of inordinate beauty. I realize this now, looking back.

That night Philip said, "Anne, I love you."

I loved him very, very much, but I would not say it. I was afraid to, maybe, fearful of putting the fact into words, of speaking it out loud for the fates to hear. Or maybe, being a woman, I was just being coy.

"I love you," he said again.

I knew that I had to do something or he would think I'd gone deaf. So I kissed him. I kissed him longer than I meant to and differently than I meant to, and when I drew back, he took a deep breath and kissed me again. My blood was racing and, between kisses, I could hear Philip's short, irregular breathing. I gathered up all my will power and tried to pull away.

"Stop it," I said. "You've got to go home."

He held me very close and kissed me once more.

"Stop it," I repeated.

"Darling, darling," he said softly. "I love you so very much."

"Go home," I said. "You've got to go home."

He let me go then. He straightened his glasses and wiped off the lipstick. He smiled, but it was a weak smile. He looked crestfallen.

"Go home," I said, grinning at him. "But come back. Oh, my dear, come back very soon."

The next day being Sunday, I rose early and went to early Communion in Van Buren and later, because the weather was still very fine, I put on some slacks and a cardigan and sat on a bench near the summerhouse in the autumn sun. I was reading the morning paper when I heard a footstep and looked up and Emily was there. She was in the same outfit she had worn that day in Tavean's room, or rather, one almost like it, but this time the shorts and socks were green. Seeing her with her knees bare and her breasts declaring themselves inside the shirt irritated me a little. I said hello to her and let my paper rustle.

She nodded and said good morning and sat down on the bench.

So I could not read my paper. I could not be that rude, but I was here first and I felt that I did not have to open the conversation. I did not have to speak.

After a little silence she said, "I was glad to see Philip Holcomb last night. He is nice. I like him. Don't you?"

Maybe if I had had a sister, my sister would have said something like this to me, and maybe I would have been content to discuss with my sister the affairs of my heart. But Emily was not my sister. She was my stepmother, as Tavean had once grossly pointed out, and whether I was in love with Philip or not was none of her business.

But I had to answer. I said, "Yes, I was glad to see him."

There was another pause while Emily looked down at her feet. She gazed at the polished loafers, then raised her eyes and folded her hands in her lap. "I knew a boy like Philip once," she said. "Not like him really, but enough so that Philip reminds me of him. They talk the same way, and Bob—that was his name—wore glasses, too."

I remember thinking that Emily must have forgotten, temporarily, who I was; that through some lapse of her intellect she must have separated me, the girl on the bench, from my identity as Father's daughter. Why else would she fail to sense my annoyance at her and at her recent behavior with Tavean and at the clothes she was wearing? Why else would she dare speak to me of the affections of her past?

I looked at her for a moment and when I spoke my voice was almost under control. I spoke almost evenly, but not quite. To my own ears my words were edged with acerbity. "Did he love you?" I asked.

"No," she replied. "But he said he did. He said he loved me and I almost married him."

Now she did not need prompting. She went on. "It was not long after I got out of high school, and he was a boy who worked for an advertising agency in the same building where I worked, and he dated me for a long time. For months we went out together and he said he loved me. Then, finally, after we had been dating almost every night for I don't know how long and he had been saying how much he loved me every time we were together, he said he wanted to marry me, and then, finally, he gave me a ring. But he did not marry me. He got another job and moved to St. Louis. He wrote me a few letters, but not very many, and not long after he had left Nashville he married a girl up there. I remember seeing her picture in the paper. She had been to Stephens."

But still I did not know what she was trying to say to me. And, unhappily, she chose this moment to cross her legs, to lift one bare knee and cross it over the other. The shorts pulled up to show more flesh, to expose a few inches of her softly rounded thigh.

So I said, "Emily, tell me something. How does it feel to be so damned beautiful?"

The color rose to Emily's face. For the first time in my life I saw her blush, and she gazed at the ground and shook her head, her lips pressed together.

"I mean it," I said. "Tell me. I'd like to know."

I said this, but of course I did not expect an answer. I thought she would collect her own anger and call me a bitch or, maybe, turn the other cheek and tell me I knew already being beautiful myself, which would be a big enough lie to end the conversation.

But her reply was, "It is like what I have just been telling you. Like what I just said. Maybe," Emily continued, "it would have been different if I had had something else. Some talent or some sense or something to go along with my face and figure. But if I did have anything, nobody ever discovered it. They would ask me to marry them sometimes, but they never loved me."

I spoke, not out of pity for her, but out of fear and sorrow for the rest of us—for myself and Tavean and Father.

"Father loves you," I said.

"Yes," she said smiling, "I know he does." But, like her voice, the smile conveyed doubt and not conviction.

I said, "He is just worried now. He is concerned over what the vandals did in the cemetery."

"Yes," she said again, "I know that. He is worried about the grave of General Adams."

She got up and started toward the house. She went across the lawn through the clear blue day, moved slowly till she came to the end of the walk. Then she followed the walk past the cemetery fence to the back veranda.

5
The Life and Times of Horatio Adams

On the day after Halloween, I went with Anne and McMurtry to the cemetery to look at my grandfather's tombstone, and when I got back to Adams' Rest, Emily was gone. I was overwrought and tired, I suppose, drained out by Tavean's accident and the vandalism in the graveyard; but I remember that when I went into the bedroom and did not find Emily, a great and unreasonable fear clutched my heart. I stopped just inside the doorway. The room was in semidarkness. The blinds were drawn and the tester of the bed cast a long shadow so that I could not tell at once whether Emily was lying there. Then my eyes grew accustomed to the dimness and I could make out the rumpled counterpane, the depression in the pillow, but the bed, like the rest of the room, was empty. I called Emily's name.

"Emily," I said and there was no echo, but the word seemed to hang for a moment in the gloomy air. Then I called to her again, and again got no answer. I went and looked in the empty dressing room and bath.

It is strange how one loss will make you fearful of another. My departure for the cemetery had been hasty. I had not consulted with Emily, I had not told her where I was going. And certainly it is not unusual for a man to come home in the afternoon and find his wife away. But I had been to the cemetery and looked at the painted headstone and, standing there at the resting place of my grandfather, I had felt more than anger. I had felt the sorrow of deprivation. I had felt like a man who has been cheated, robbed of one of the things he holds most dear. Now, unreasonably, I feared that I had lost Emily, too.

It passed quickly. I remember the one quick thrust of panic, the shock that ran to the raw nerve ends, and then weakly, trembling a little, I came to my senses. I made my way to the bed and lay down on it. I lay in the darkened room and thought of the desecrated headstone, and after a while I drifted off to sleep.

When I awakened, Emily had come back. She had turned on a light and she was sitting with her bare foot propped up on a stool, polishing her toenails.

"Oh, you're awake," she said. "Anne told me what happened. I'm sorry, Horatio."

"What did Anne tell you?"

"About the cemetery," she replied. "I saw the soldier. I drove in to see how Tavean was doing, and then coming home, I went by the drugstore on the square."

"How is Tavean?"

"He was still sleeping," she said. "But he looked better to me. His color has improved."

For a moment I watched her in silence. She finished one foot and went to work on the other one.

"Emily," I said, "why do you suppose they did it?"

"What?" she replied. Then she remembered. "Oh, the painting. To be funny. For a joke."

She smiled. "The soldier is kind of funny, Horatio. They were wrong to go to the cemetery, but I laughed when I saw the soldier. There were a lot of children playing around him, having a good time."

"Funny?" I said. "You thought it was funny?"

"Yes," she replied, "a little. Didn't you?"

I sat up on the bed and stared at her, the figure leaning gracefully toward the lamplight, her hand carefully busy above her toes. I was hurt that she so little understood the meaning of the vandalism and then I was angry. I rose and lit a cigarette and stood by the mantelpiece puffing deeply, but Emily did not look up. She did not seem to realize that she had said anything to offend me, and after a while I got the anger under control. My hand was still shaking but I was able to think more clearly, and it occurred to me that she simply didn't understand about the past. She knew about the present. She could understand about Tavean's accident or about Anne's attachment to Philip Holcomb, but she couldn't understand about my grandfather. Or me, I thought, with the hurt and the anger both returning. If she doesn't see why I love my grandfather, how can she love me?

"Emily," I said sharply, "don't be a fool. Be young and innocent, but try to remember that you're human. Don't think you're going to live forever, because you're not."

She regarded me in startled silence, her lips slightly parted, her eyes wide.

"You think that, don't you?" I said.

"I don't even know what you're talking about."

"You do," I insisted. "You think I'm an old man and maybe, being old, I ought to think about the dead and about dying. But not you. You're young and death is very far away from you and the dead don't matter."

She jumped out of her chair, her eyes flashing. "Don't tell me what I think! You don't know what I think! You're not a mind reader!"

"Don't be silly," I said. "Anybody would know what you're thinking. You don't give a damn about the desecration of the monuments. That doesn't mean anything to you. But Tavean's accident, that's different, isn't it? You go down to the clinic just to sit in the room with him and watch him sleep."

"Horatio!" she said, her voice shocked into softness. "Oh, Horatio!" She sat down again and covered her face with her hands. There was a moment of silence. Then I began to feel guilty and very much ashamed.

"I'm sorry," I said. "I didn't mean that. I didn't mean for it to sound that way." I went to her and put my arm around her shoulder. "Emily, Emily," I said, "I am sorry. I didn't mean what you think I meant. Please try to understand."

She was crying. She kept her face in her hands and said nothing.

"Come here," I said, taking her arm and lifting her up as gently as I could. "Come sit beside me. I've got to explain it to you. You must see what I meant."

We sat down on the bed and I took her hand which was cold and wet with her tears.

"My dear," I said, "I know it is unpleasant to think of,

but we are all going to die. I am going to die a long time before you do but you will die, too, someday, and when you are as old as I am it is hard to think about death because you do not want to die; there is too much to live for. "You are very beautiful. And you will still be beautiful ten years from now when I am sixty-seven and you will still be handsome twenty years from now when I will most likely be dead. But if I am not dead then, think what an old man I will be and how much of life's pleasure I will have lost and how much less then your handsomeness will mean to me."

"Don't," she said. "Don't talk about death."

"Listen," I said. "I have got to talk about it. We must grow old. We must die. And sometimes in bed at night, it comes to me that another day is gone, another segment of life has passed, and I am that much closer to having to leave you. Oh, then, it is a great comfort to have you near me in the night, and loving you is a great comfort and a great pain, because finally by death, love must be broken. Darling, darling, I must talk to you about death, because death is not just something that is coming. It exists now, it is now, it is a part of life, an aspect of living. And what small consolation have we, except the hope that we might live on in memory?"

I paused. Then I said, "Live on in the memory of man, endure in the recollection of the living. Don't you see now? My grandfather was an Adams and we are Adams' too and my hope has been that we all might be remembered."

She had grown very pale. There was no question now of

tears. She was beyond weeping. Her hand lay very limp in mine and her white face showed nothing.

After a while I said, "Emily, I am sorry I lost my temper."

"It's all right," she replied thinly. "I'm sorry whoever it was painted . . . " But she could not finish. For some reason she could not bring herself to name the marker of a grave. She rose and walked to the shadows near the window. She stood with her back to the room, her eyes toward the outside darkness. I saw her reach up and smooth her hair with her hands, and once I thought I heard her sigh, but the sound was very soft and I could not be certain. At last, she came back toward the lamplight, passed by me with her eyes averted, and sat down in a chair. Barefooted, dressed in a simple skirt and blouse, she looked very young and very pretty, and I knew that I loved her very much.

"Emily," I said, "I love you."

I walked to her and leaned down but she did not look at me. I raised her chin and kissed her and she did not avoid my kiss. But her lips, warm and soft as they were, were not responsive. They lay flat and dry against her teeth. They received my kiss with no show of life, no quickening of emotion.

"Darling," I said insistently, "I do love you."

Still she made no reply and I should have stopped here, I should have left her alone. But I could not stop anymore than the sky could halt the sun, or the clock on the mantelpiece could cease its ticking. I kissed her again and this time she tried, and later back on the bed she tried. She went coldly, but as best she could, I suppose, through passion's motions. When it was over and I moved away, she pulled her skirt down to cover her thighs. She lay very still with her head turned away from me.

I know that though I had tried very hard, I had not succeeded in explaining what I felt to Emily. There are some things in life which are very simple, there are concatenations which are very easy to comprehend. A few days later, in his room downstairs, Tavean lay in his bed with a broken ankle. He could point to the cast at the end of his leg and say, "It is here, inside this that I hurt, and the pain is the result of a blow which was the result of an accident."

But what is the quality of grief? What is the locus of bereavement's pain? What organ feels the sense of loss most sharply? In the time of sorrow, we speak of a broken heart, but to speak so is to use an image, a correlative based on a physiological misconception. On the morning after the twenty-seventh anniversary of my marriage to Nancy, I broke into the sunlit bedroom to look upon the loved face which was the face of death. And you do not love the face of death, because it is no longer the living face, but the living face still exists to be loved in the chambers of memory. For me, when Nancy died, there was the pain of loss, there was the pain of my own death which was forecast by hers, there was pain for the pain that I knew would be felt by Anne and Tavean. And beyond this was the guilt, imperfectly realized but real none the less. For in the case of suicide, who within the ambiance of the victim's life can count himself guiltless?

On All Saints' Eve, Anne had gone to the church and

prayed for Nancy. She had lighted a candle and knelt in her pew, and this is the best way to remember the dead, if you can truly believe in the efficacy of prayers and candles. But I could not believe, not enough anyway, and not believing I could not pray, but I did not sufficiently not believe to stay far from the altar. It is one thing to have faith by which you can live, and another thing to have no faith and let your strength be yourself; but to be like me and to have little faith is to suffer the curse of man from the time of the serpent. This perhaps is what I should have said to Emily.

But I did not say this, and after that day in the bedroom, after our cold and determined passion, our lives were never quite the same again. I know that in the early weeks of our marriage, when we had just returned from our honeymoon and were living in the house in Nashville, I would go to town in the morning with the recollection of Emily's beauty fresh in my mind. Through the day I would think of her and long for the night when I would see her, and sometimes I would call her on the phone. Then later, when the working time was over, my heart would beat with urgency as I drove through the evening traffic out the Harding Road.

At Adams' Rest it was different. I would think frequently of Emily, but there were other things which crowded into my mind and demanded my attention. In the mornings, on the way to the city, I would pass the statue which had been cleaned now, but which still reminded me of the vandals. Anger would invade my thoughts and, temporarily at least, my sense of love would be overshadowed. Often, in town, I would wonder how

McMurtry was progressing in his investigation of the vandalism; and I would pass the statue on my way back home and arrive sometimes sorrowful and petulant. Emily would be in the room with Tavean, but usually she would hear me coming, catch the sound of the car on the drive or the soft jar of the closing front door, and she would come out into the hall to greet me. Seeing her, I would feel the race of my blood. I would kiss her there in the hall and she would walk up the stairs with me.

At Adams' Rest, unless we were having company for dinner—and during that time the company was always Philip Holcomb—we wore very informal clothing, even when we dined. I would take off the suit I had worn for business and put on a pair of slacks and a sport shirt and, while I changed my clothes, Emily sat on the love seat or leaned against the sill of one of the windows or lay down, sometimes, on the tester bed. Looking back, I know that she tried very hard to divert my mind from the gloomy thoughts the sight of the statue always occasioned in me. She would tell me what she and Tavean had talked about. Or she would tell me about a movie she had seen on television. Or she would show me an advertisement of a dress in a magazine. Or she would ask me what I had been doing and whether the market had closed up or down. I would respond to her as politely, as lovingly as I could, but sooner or later I was bound to fall into a silence or to change the subject and begin to talk of my grandfather's stone.

One evening not long after Tavean's accident, Emily suggested that we might go back to Nashville. She was standing near the hearth in the bedroom. A fire was burning and I saw her figure darkly against the firelight; the narrow waist, the flaring folds of the full skirt.

"Darling," she said, "why don't we go back to Nashville? Tavean doesn't need us anymore."

These are the words that she used and they were innocent enough, but the tone of her voice conveyed some further meaning. She spoke too brightly, with too great an air of casualness, as if the question of our leaving Adams' Rest were of no particular significance, and as if before this moment, she had not previously considered whether we ought to remain here or go.

"My dear," I said, "we are not staying here because of Tavean only. I want to keep behind McMurtry. If I leave, he will simply forget about the vandalism. He will sit down and quit working on the case."

"But there are other things more important than . . ." she said, and then broke off suddenly.

"Than what?" I asked.

She did not answer.

"Than what, Emily?"

She moved toward me and stopped very close to me, her brown eyes wide open and peering into mine. "Darling," she said, "please, darling. Oh, Horatio, please take me home."

There were times when Emily appeared very young to me; when her face seemed as smooth and innocent as the innocent face of a child and when her voice had the simple ring of a child's greeting.

Now she seemed very young indeed, and I put my arm around her shoulder and patted her shoulder affectionately, and said, "My dear, this is your home. It is the real home, the oldest home for all of us."

"No, no," she replied, her tone almost desperate. "That is not what I meant. Let's go back to the other house, to the one in Nashville."

"Not yet," I replied. "I cannot go yet. I have told you why."

Strangely, or seen in recollection, not strangely, for nothing is strange in the following light of understanding; curiously to me then, Anne also suggested that Emily and I should leave Adams' Rest. It was one Sunday morning when Anne had been to the movies with Philip Holcomb the night before and then had risen early to go to church. When she found me alone in the living room where I was drinking coffee, I thought that she suffered only from a want of sleep. She was wearing slacks and a sweater, and she bade me good morning a little shortly and refused my invitation to sit down. She stood with her back to the front windows, her hands in her pockets. She looked around the room as if she wanted to make sure no one else was present and, at last, she let her gaze come to rest on me. She told me that she thought I ought to take Emily back to Nashville, and I was struck with the fact that when she spoke of the house in Belle Meade, she used the same word Emily had used—she referred to it as home.

"Father," Anne said, "you ought to take Emily home."

I explained to Anne why I could not do this and then I said, "This is home or ought to be more of a home for Emily. The other house was built for your mother. It was put up according to her design."

"That does not matter," Anne said, her voice edged with annoyance. "Emily is not jealous of Mother. She does not care."

"All right," I replied sharply, "that does not matter. But neither is it the point. I intend to see that whoever painted the graves is punished. I care about what has happened, whether anybody else does or not."

"You care about yourself!" she said. "That's what you care about! You don't give a simple damn for anything else!"

She turned away from me. We had both been speaking rather loudly. Now the room was quiet, filled with silence and autumn sunlight, and Anne's shadow was cast long upon the floor. I took a sip of my coffee and the saucer clinked against the cup.

Finally Anne faced me again and said, "I am sorry, Father. I did not mean to say that. It is not true. But you keep on worrying about the past and future, and there is nobody attending to the present. You are planning on what will happen to us when we are all dead, but who will see after us now when we are alive?"

"Little Anne," I said, for Tavean called her this sometimes and I had picked it up from him as a term of affection. "I will see after you if I can possibly do it. Little Anne, tell me what's wrong."

"Nothing," she said, "oh, nothing. I don't know what to tell you. I don't really know."

So, Emily longed to return to the city and Anne longed for me to take her there; and every morning I rose and went to work, thinking sometimes of Emily and less often of Anne, and thinking, studying most of all about the vandals. As the days passed, Tavean began to recover and soon he was able to leave his bed and walk on crutches. One night I sat alone with him in the library, which was one of my favorite rooms at Adams' Rest. There were not many books because no one had added to the collection after my Grandfather Adams went to the Civil War. But, of course, the books that were there were old, and the furniture was old. The lamps were the old ones that had been converted to electricity, and the carpet and draperies, though not the originals, were in the old fashion. To go into the house at Adams' Rest was, in a way, to go into another time; but of all the corners of the premises, this room most bespoke the past and bespoke it most eloquently.

Tavean sat with his crutches at his side, his injured limb stretched awkwardly before him. His face was pale from his days spent inside, but except for this, he looked healthy enough, and handsome with his short, black, slightly curly hair, and his dark eyes that were so much like Nancy's.

"I am going to Nashville tomorrow," he said. "I think I could drive it myself if I tried. But I suppose I will get one of the men on the place here to drive me."

I cannot say that I was truly sorry. For a moment I felt a twinge of apprehension. I think I had always been oversolicitous of my children, and particularly of Tavean. For one brief second, it was in my mind to protest, to argue that his hurt would not permit the journey. Then too, I was disappointed, in a fashion, that he, like Emily and Anne, did not feel bound to remain near the cemetery until the vandals who had painted the stone were caught.

But I know that most of all I was relieved that he and Emily would, for a while at least, be separated, and I would have one less worry on my mind.

"Do you feel like it?" I asked. "Are you up to going?"

He nodded.

"Then there is no need to bother any of the men," I said. "I'll go in tomorrow. Why don't you ride with me?"

"No," he said, "I've got one leg left which is all you need to drive with. I'd like to have a car with me, when I get back home."

I half rose to move toward the hall. I was on the point of saying good night when Tavean's voice arrested me.

"Father," he said, "you ought to go back to Nashville, too. You ought to take Emily."

So now he had taken up the refrain and, though I had not understood Emily's motives when she had asked to go home, and had comprehended Anne's reasons even more imperfectly, for the moment, at least, I believed I knew what Tavean had in mind. I was jealous of Tavean. It occurred to me that now that he was mobile, he wanted room to move in, a city where, with a little discretion, he might take Emily about and hope not to stir up gossip, start loose talk.

"I do not want to go to Nashville," I said. "And I do not want to take Emily there."

I paused. Then I said, "You do not have to go, either. If you will miss our company, then you are free to stay here and enjoy it. But I will decide where Emily will be better off."

"Then why don't you think about her?" he said firmly,

but softly; his temper, like Nancy's, had been always a little more even than mine.

"I do," I replied sharply. "I will. And I suggest that you think less about her." I rose and took a few steps toward the doorway. "It's none of your business, Tavean," I said. "She is my wife. You leave her to me."

Then I moved into the hall and mounted the steps.

The next morning when I was having breakfast with Anne, Mr. McMurtry called me on the telephone. I took the call in the dining room and his voice came briskly over the instrument.

"This is McMurtry," he said. "I've got something else to report about that monument."

"You've caught them?" I asked.

"No, sir," he said, some of the old army crispness going out of his voice. "It's not exactly that. They come again last night and done some more painting."

"They what?" I said.

"Yes, sir," he replied. "They painted the soldier's coat red and his britches blue. They put red and blue stripes on his face. He looks like an Indian."

I said, "And you don't have one idea in the world who in the hell is doing it."

"I'm working on it," he said. "It's some boys here in the neighborhood, but they do it at night, and I don't even know that the statue's been painted till daylight."

That was apparently all he could say. By his own words he defined his incompetence, with his own voice he measured his failure as a police officer. But what good would it do to point this out to him now?

"Have you been to the cemetery?" I asked, my voice trembling.

"Yes, sir," he said. He paused again.

I said, "Well?"

"Yes, sir," he repeated. "They done the marker over too. It's painted up with flowers like a piece of wallpaper."

I hung up the phone and turned to look at Anne and I believe I studied her face for a long time in silence. I sat and gazed at her rounded chin, her freshly rouged lips, her dark hair, and eyebrows. Then I said, "That was Mc-Murtry." I struck the table with my open hand, and said more loudly, "God damn it, they have done it again!"

"Paint?" she asked.

I nodded.

"I'm sorry," she said. "I am truly sorry, Father."

"Sorry, hell!" I replied.

"Father," Anne said sternly, "I am sorry."

"All right," I said, "I'm sorry, too, but that doesn't help matters. That doesn't take the paint off the stone or catch the vandals."

"No," she said, "it doesn't."

Then she said, "Tavean and Emily will be sorry, too."

I did not reply. I went out and got in my car and drove to town and saw the statue. Then I drove out to the cemetery and the marker looked exactly as McMurtry had said it looked. It was covered with rather neatly drawn red and blue flowers, like the design on a cheap and garish piece of wallpaper. I examined the stone for a little while and thought of my grandfather who had died near this town on a day when this town and the fathers of these people were living under an enemy occupation. I thought of the time not long ago when the name of Tavean Adams had meant something and when the recollection of the Confederacy and of the Confederate Army had been kept brightly alive.

Well, I said, not really talking, but saying the words over in my mind, *they have done it again and it will have to be cleaned again, but this is the last damn time they are going to do it.*

So the first thing I did when I got to Nashville was to call my lawyer. I told him I wanted to move my grandfather's body from the Confederate cemetery to the private burial ground at Adams' Rest. Later in the morning, he came to see me at my office.

He was a man about my age or maybe a few years older, tall and gray and conservatively dressed, and his name was Harry Livingston. The Livingstons were very prominent in middle Tennessee. They had been prominent for many generations, and Harry's Grandfather Livingston had been on the staff of one of the generals in the Army of Northern Virginia. I knew this because I had been acquainted with Harry for a long time. He had always been my attorney and I often saw him at meetings of the Historical Society.

He sat down and rested his hand on the edge of my desk, drummed his fingers on the desk top, and said, "Horatio, what in the name of goodness are you up to?"

He knew of course about the Halloween vandalism. That had been in the Nashville newspapers. Now I told him what had been done last night, and I told him that I intended to remove my grandfather's body from its public place among a people who treated the monument and what the monument stood for with so little respect.

"Horatio," he said, gazing at me with very bright blue, very young-looking eyes, "you know me. You know where I stand and how I feel about General Adams."

"Yes," I replied, "I know."

"Then take my advice," he said. "Forget about this thing, painful as it is. Forget what a few thoughtless boys have done and let all this blow over."

"You don't understand it," I said. "Has anybody ever marked up your grandfather's stone?"

"No," he replied. "But I believe if someone did, I wouldn't make too much of it. I wouldn't give the vandals the satisfaction of seeing me in a rage."

"That's not the point," I said. I was growing a little angry and I did not want to discuss the question with him. "Tell me what I've got to do to open the grave."

He argued no more. He nodded his head and opened his briefcase and took out a piece of paper, a printed form. It was an Application for Disinterment Permit and it was a relatively simple form which required only the signature of the county health officer.

"Now," Harry said, "the best thing to do is to do this thing quietly and to do it quick. Don't trifle with the form yourself. Take it to an undertaker—one in Nashville so there will be no chance of gossip getting started before you are ready to act. Have the undertaker come down to Van Buren one morning ready to go to work. He can go to the county health officer in the Van Buren courthouse, and the health officer will have to sign, because he will have no reason for not signing and no grounds on which to delay signing. Then you go get the body and you have the other grave open already and you put the body in the other grave and cover it up. I tell you to do it this way, because if you get the permit signed one day and plan on getting the body the next, there will be time for somebody to go to court and maybe get an injunction against you. Then we'll be lawing and setting precedents for the rest of our lives."

He paused. "We may be lawing over this for the rest of our lives anyway, but you'll have the body while we do."

"All right," I said, "and I thank you."

He shut his briefcase and got up. Then from the doorway he said, "Horatio, you're going to let the undertaker handle the whole thing, aren't you? I mean, you aren't going along to help or watch?"

"Certainly I mean to go," I said. "Why shouldn't I?"

"Well," he replied, "in a public business such as this where there are likely to be hard feelings, it is best to keep yourself in the background as much as you can."

"I'm not worried about that," I said. "The hard feelings on my side needn't be kept secret."

When Harry left, I began to think about an undertaker, and the first one that came into my mind was the one who had buried Nancy. I did not really want to go to him because of my memory of Nancy's funeral, but I knew him and he knew me, and I believed I could trust him to do what I told him to do with dispatch and discretion. After lunch, I drove out to the funeral parlor.

The undertaker's name was Mr. Rathbone. I had not called to make an appointment with him, partly because I did not think an appointment would be necessary with an undertaker, and partly because I had taken very seriously Harry Livingston's advice to keep my intention secret as long as I could. I drove out West End Avenue, found a parking place, and walked half a block back to the big old house that had once been a residence, but which had been modified, added on to, and remodeled until its rooms now accommodated the demands of Mr. Rathbone's trade.

At most funeral homes, when there is a funeral in progress, the hearse will be parked out in front, and there will be a policeman on a motorcycle waiting to lead the procession, and two or three limousines will be parked behind the hearse. At Mr. Rathbone's, however, there was a wide concrete driveway that ran up by the side of the house and a side entrance where the casket could be carried out to the hearse that waited in the shelter of a porte-cochere. But I did not know this when I went to call on Mr. Rathbone. Nancy had lain in state at home and her body had been taken from our house to the church for her funeral services.

I went up the walk, opened the door, and moved inside into the sound of music. Perhaps if the music had been the music you would expect, one of the old gospel hymns that are played at funerals, I might have guessed what was going on before I made my entry. If the sound I heard had been the sound of an organ, I might not have fully opened the door and stepped with confidence across the threshold. But the music was foreign to my ears. It was symphonic music, but not the symphonic music that I am accustomed to. It was not Mozart or Beethoven or Wagner. Whatever it was, I suppose it was meant to be sad, and in the harshness of its discords, the perversities of its rhythms, it was mournful in its way, but it was not music that I wanted to listen to or that I would ever like. Raucously, the sound burst from an amplifier near the door.

I had come into a large central hallway and to my right was a long room, what most likely had been two rooms when the home was a residence. Here, folding chairs had been set up in close rows; there were people sitting on the chairs and at the front of the room there was a coffin. On the other side of the hall there was a kind of lounge; there were people here, too, and people were milling about, coming and going in the hallway. A man in a red necktie and a brown tweed jacket, a tall man with thick, black hair, a pale face, and bad teeth, came up to me and looked at me questioningly and shook my hand.

"Wouldn't you like to sign the register?" he said, his voice loud to carry above the music.

"No," I replied, "I just came to see Mr. Rathbone."

Apparently, the tall man did not understand me.

"It's all right," he insisted rudely. "It won't hurt you to write your name, will it? Considering all that's happened I think Lavinia will want to know who came."

I shook my head and moved away from him. I walked not back out the door where a more sensible or a less harassed man would have gone, but having got this far and having suffered this much embarrassment, I walked the length of the hallway toward the offices that I knew to be at the rear. I moved through the noise of that awful music, paced in full view of this strange group of mourners, and came at last to a smaller room furnished with a glass-topped desk and a few chairs, a chromium smoking stand, and here and there on the walls a few noncommital pictures. Behind the desk sat a young man with a wide, flat face. Wearing a dark suit, a figured tie, he was dressed with the not quite shabby neatness of a funeral parlor factotum. I told the young man that I wanted to see Mr. Rathbone.

Mr. Rathbone was busy with the funeral, but the young man, who said his name was Roberts, told me that the funeral would not last very long. The body was to be sent out of town for cremation, and Mr. Rathbone would not likely accompany it to the train. So Roberts and I waited in the office and the sound of the service came to us clearly from the other room. We listened for a while to the music. Then the music stopped and the voice of a man I could not see filled the silence. First, the man in the next room read a poem which I remembered from my youth and which begins, "Out of the night that covers me, Black as the pit from pole to pole, I thank WHATEVER GODS MAY BE, For my unconquerable soul." That is the way he read it, coming down heavily on the questionable character of the gods. Then he read two or three other poems in the same vein, poems which celebrated the courage of man, and then he made a speech to the assembled company.

It was a very personal speech; in a way, it was similar to the sermons I used to hear at Protestant funerals when I was very young. The deceased man's name was Paul. Paul had been an artist, a painter, and the speaker told how he had met Paul and admired him. He spoke of Paul's courage and compared him to the prophets of old who had stood up firmly for the sake of the new truth, as Paul had stood up for the new aesthetic truth in his painting.

"*Ars est omnia*," the speaker said. "In a very real sense,

art is all. What greater legacy can a man leave than a legacy of beauty? By what surer means than through the creation of art can a man leave his mark upon the world and gain the signal immortality of being ever remembered, ever cherished in the minds of all succeeding generations? We do not know what comes after death. We do not know whether there is another life or not, or if there is another life, what shape that life may take. Nor do we know whether it is best to be among the dead, or to remain, as you and I remain today, among the living. Those of us who mourn may take small comfort from this uncertainty; but we may take great comfort indeed, in our memory of a life well lived, a death well met, a fame which will be made more and more secure by the future's judgement. As long as man has eyes to see and the brain and the heart to comprehend, Paul shall be remembered."

The voice stopped. The speaker was finished. I thought that perhaps there would be some kind of prayer, but there was no prayer. The music took up again and played while the casket was carried to the hearse. The funeral was over.

I sat and thought about what I had heard and considered the strangeness of the funeral service. I thought how painful death was, and what little encouragement the speaker had been able to give Paul's widow, if he had left a widow, or to his children or his parents or his brothers and sisters, if he had had any of these.

I turned to look at Roberts, but his wide face was placid. He showed no emotion, neither sadness nor surprise. He had taken out his pen and a piece of paper. He was writing a letter.

"That was a curious service," I said.

He smiled. "I guess it might sound that way, sir," he said, "if you had never been to this kind of funeral."

"Yes," I replied weakly, "I guess so."

Then Mr. Rathbone was with us in the office. He greeted me very courteously. He said it would be a privilege to serve me in any way that he could.

6
The Recollections of Anne Adams

I suppose the moment comes in everybody's life when he would like to play God and know, at a given moment in time, the secret feelings of another human heart, the secret thoughts another brain is thinking. During that fall when we were at Adams' Rest, I would have welcomed the opportunity to see into the consciousness of Father or of Emily, but as time passed, as the days drew out to make weeks and the weeks carried us on into December, I wanted most of all to know about Tavean and what images filled his mind's waking silence.

It was not often that I was able to see him alone. As I have said, in the mornings and in the afternoons, Emily was often with him; in his room before he was able to leave his bed, moving with him about the house after he learned to use his crutches. But there were odd hours when I would go in to see Tavean, in his room or later in the library or in the living room when we could be alone together for a few minutes. Then it would sometimes be like the old days before Mother killed herself, before we knew of the existence of Emily, before whoever did it had painted the soldier on the square.

For me, it was always easy to talk to Tavean. I think this was because to me, at least, he was always very considerate. He never treated me as other boys treated their little sisters, as annoyances that were better left at home, worrisome brats that might happily be forgotten. In the summers of our youth, Tavean would take me fishing sometimes, and he took me to the river and taught me to water ski. More than once when I was in high school, he allowed me to double date with him, arranged the double date when he knew that the boy I was going out with was too young to drive.

I learned the minor vices from Tavean. I began smoking his cigarettes and the first drink I ever had was made with his whiskey. He joyfully encouraged me to do the things that Father and Mother had forbidden me to do, because, he said, it was everybody's duty to have a good time and be happy. Once I pointed out to him that Father and Mother would be hurt if they found out I took a drink, and he replied only that they must not find out. They would be happy as long as they did not know what I was doing. I would be happy doing what I wanted to do.

That was the way Tavean looked at life. He believed in human happiness as other people believe in God. Or, to put it another way, he was haunted by the joyful prospect of living, just as Father was haunted by the thought of death. In the time following his accident, I would be alone with Tavean late in the afternoon when

Father had come home from town and before he and Emily had come back downstairs for dinner.

Tavean would be in his bed and he would look at me and smile and say, "Little Anne, do you remember that winter in Florida when I got so awfully sunburned on the beach?" Or he would gaze out at the autumn twilight and speak of a hunt he had been on with Father. Or he would talk of a football game he had seen on television or a book he had read.

While he was in the house with nothing to do, he began to work crossword puzzles and he was continually coming across a new word, a new name for a commonplace thing, or a new verb or adjective he had never before heard of. He would tell me of his discoveries with great glee, and from his bed, or later from his chair in the library, or in the living room, he would practice using the new word in a sentence. He would take great delight in springing the word on Philip, who was, Tavean said laughingly, a professor and who should know about everything and what everything meant.

As soon as he was able to use his crutches, Tavean went out on the porch and breathed the air of the morning. He would pick up a maple leaf that had fallen and look at it, or he would pluck a blade of the dying grass and chew on the stem.

He loved life and he lived as if life were never going to end, or as if it were going to end tomorrow. I suppose that in the final analysis Mother was right when she said Tavean was like Father, and it is possible that if I had been able to play God that autumn and look into the secret chambers of Tavean's heart, I would have found there the same concern, the same fearful demon which possessed Father. Maybe Father and Tavean were the same and only acted or reacted differently, but of this who can be certain? Who can know?

Tavean loved life and this was well, except that a part of the life he loved was Emily. I think, through all the happy moments I spent with Tavean, I was always conscious of Emily's existence, and often enough she was alone with Tavean or present with both of us in the flesh. She would be in the room with us, her pretty clothes clinging snugly or draping neatly over her body, and her Joy or Chanel or Odalisque filling the air. She moved in an aura of sweetness which was the perfume that she wore, but I do not believe that Tavean was ever fully aware that her scent came from a bottle. In his fond bemusement, his delight in her presence, he seemed to believe that whatever he smelled, whatever it was that pleased his nostrils, was only the natural emanation of Emily's living state. Oh, he loved her, he must have loved her, just as he apparently loved everything else that he ever saw.

He loved Emily, but the question was how much did he love her? And what did he mean to do about his love for her? And how much was his love for her increasing day by day? I know that I was not the only one to suggest to Father that he take Emily home. Tavean suggested that Father take her home, too, and when Father refused, then Tavean said he, himself, would leave. But he did not leave because of the second act of vandalism. On the morning after the vandals had painted the statue for the second time, Tavean came into the breakfast room just after Father had left and I told him what had happened and he seemed very much concerned. His forehead wrinkled, his eyes narrowed. He sat down in silence, lowered himself into a chair awkwardly and laid his crutches on the floor. Then he said, "Damn it, they picked a hell of a time to do it. Now I'll have to stay here a few days longer."

"Were you going home?" I asked.

"I was," he replied, "but I can't go now."

I thought about this for a while. I served Tavean's breakfast from the sideboard in the dining room, brought the plate to him, set it down before him, poured his coffee, and then resumed my seat. "Why?" I said at last. "Why can't you go home?"

"Why?" he said. "Why, because of Father. He'll be raging around here like a mad bull for the next week."

I said, "You can't stop that by staying here."

"No," he replied. He paused. Then he went on, "I just thought it might be hard on Emily. She might need some help."

"Tavean," I said flatly, "are you in love with Emily?"

He looked hard at me across the table, his face tense and almost angry. The muscles of his jaws gathered, the skin on his cheeks grew rigid; then he seemed to relax a little, and he said, "Little Anne, you know how Father is. You love him and I love him, but we know how he is."

"Yes," I replied pointedly, "I know about Father. I guess Emily is the one I don't understand."

"Damn it!" Tavean said, "look at what Father is doing to Emily. Don't you remember Mother and what he did to her?"

This was too much, this linking together of Mother and Emily; this comparison of Emily's present discomfort, whatever it was, to the last days of Mother's life and to her years with Father which, in a way, had prepared for these days and prepared for her death. It was too much to hear Mother's name spoken in the same breath with that of Emily, but it was no less, I suppose, than I deserved. For after all, I had been the one who had almost said to Father, *But don't you see? Don't you understand? She killed herself not because she was afraid of death or even of suffering. She killed herself because of you.* This I had almost said once to Father and would have said, except for Tavean, who had peered at me from the shadows of the library and stopped my words.

"All right," I said. "I do remember. But maybe we were wrong."

"No," Tavean said. "We were right."

"Listen," I said, "we are older now. Not much older, not even a year older, but a lot has happened since Mother was buried, a lot has happened just since we have been here at Adams' Rest. Life is not as simple as we thought it was. I have no brief for what Father did to Mother. I don't even say that he is treating Emily the way he ought to treat her. But things don't just happen for one reason. Father was wrong, but he didn't give Mother cancer, if she had cancer, and he didn't cause whatever it was in her lungs to make her sick in the first place and go to Dr. Anderson and get scared."

"Maybe so," he said, "but granted there are some things you can't help, you still ought to do what you can."

"What can you do?" I asked.

He said, "I can try to help Emily. I can try to see that Father makes her happy."

He said this as simply, as confidently, as if he were speaking of arranging a dinner menu, or of selecting a Christmas present, or of buying tickets to a play. He spoke as if life, this life that he loved so much, were a mere problem in arithmetic, a sum to add, a difference to subtract. In the midst of my wonder at his innocence, I remembered once more what Mother had said, that Tavean, like Father, could not bear suffering. They could not stand by and see others endure it.

But now, what could I say to him, what reply could I make other than to call him an idiot, a fool? So I returned to my original question. "Tell me," I said, "are you in love with Emily?"

For a moment I thought he was going to say that it was none of my business. Again his face was lined with anger, then again the face relaxed and he almost smiled. His lips softened and parted slightly and he said, "Yes, I guess I am, but you don't understand it. I guess I do love her, but it is not like you think."

And he was right about that. Try as I might—and I did try, I had been trying for a long time—I could not understand the attraction Emily held for Tavean. Sometimes in my bed at night, or in a quiet time of the afternoon, or in the stillness of morning when I had just finished breakfast, or when I was on my way home from the early Communion service in Van Buren, I would make a catalogue of all the things that I knew about Emily and try to decide why Father should have married her and why Tavean should love her. I know this was silly. I was pretty certain that I was in love with Philip, but I could not say why I loved him. If I tried to say why, even to myself, I said all the wrong things and wound up sounding like the unrhymed lyrics to a very bad song. Concerning Emily, I knew that any casting director of any chorus line could have given me an explanation. Virgin that I was and therefore practically inexperienced in the ways of love, I knew nonetheless about the birds and bees. I had read a little Freud in my time and I felt something of passion's heat when I kissed Philip. But what was happening to us, what had happened to Father to make him marry Emily, and what was happening to Tavean to make him love her would have to be something more than this. I did not doubt Emily's fleshly beauty. But if, as I had told Tavean, life was complex and the ends of life were the results of complex causes, then there must be more to Emily than thigh and breast, hips and slender waistline, and tapered ankle. Tavean was right, I did not understand. And maybe I shouldn't have tried, being only a woman.

On the night following the second night of vandalism, the evening of the day when Father had spoken harshly on the phone to Mr. McMurtry, Philip came to Adams' Rest for dinner. He and Tavean and I were in the living room drinking our martinis and our whiskey. It was dark beyond the windows. Inside the room, the lamps were burning and a fire burned in the fireplace and Tavean was trying some of his new words on Philip. He asked Philip what *inspissate* meant and Philip did not know and Tavean told him. Then Tavean tried *pogonia,* and Philip did not know what this was, either, and Tavean laughed and told Philip that he was not fit to teach and that he was going to report Philip to the university chancellor. Then Emily and Father came into the room.

I can see the two of them as they moved through the doorway, their figures halted in memory, stilled in recollection, like the characters in a pageant; Emily a step or two inside the living room and Father just behind her looking almost gay. Or perhaps gay is not the right word, for he was not smiling. His lips were pursed slightly and the handsome, somewhat tanned face seemed to be in thoughtful and determined repose, the cheeks faintly lined, the eyes very bright and glancing at each of us, at Tavean and at me, and resting finally on Philip.

Emily was very pale. She was wearing a black dress—which I thought was a little pretentious for the country—and above and beside the black silk, her skin was a pure, a dead white, and the brightness of her almost silver hair emphasized the dull whiteness of her forehead. Her hands were folded together at her waist and, at last, she managed a weak grin and she bade us good evening.

"Well," Father said, "did you hear about it, Philip?"

Even Philip knew what Father meant and he had heard. I had told him.

"Yes, sir," Philip said. "I'm mighty sorry, Horatio."

"Yes," Father said briskly, "sorry. So am I. But, by God, I'm going to fix them this time. It won't happen again."

We were all startled, I think, as much by Father's tone as by his words.

Tavean said, "How, Father? How are you going to fix them? What are you going to do?"

"Bring him here," Father said, almost triumphantly. "I am going to bring Grandfather Adams here. I mean to bury him on our own land where he will be safe from vandals."

There was a silence. I remember that I looked at Emily and understood her paleness and thought perhaps that the color was leaving my face, too. I turned then to Philip. He sat absolutely motionless, his glass half lifted to his mouth, his lips slightly parted, his eyes open wide in disbelief.

Only Tavean's face showed nothing. In a very even, very reasonable voice he said, "But there will not be much left to bring, Father. There will only be the skeleton, the loose bones."

"Oh," Emily said. It was a little gasp.

And I said, "Hush, Tavean!" For I saw it only too clearly in my mind's eye, the skeleton exposed in the brown earth, the earth being carefully removed from around the crumbling bone. The ribs rising first into view, the empty eyes filled with dirt, and the tedious digging going on to expose the old, imperfect teeth, and the feet and legs, the hands and arms, and maybe an old shred of gray cloth, a belt buckle, a few buttons.

"My God, Horatio," Phil said, "leave it alone."

"No," Father replied, shaking his head.

"What good will it do, Father?" Tavean asked.

And Father said, "I can protect him here. That's what I told you."

"Then just bring the monument home," Tavean said, "they are not likely to paint Great-grandfather."

"Tavean," Father said, "it is not funny. And I don't give a damn whether you want him brought here or not."

For a moment nobody spoke. Then Philip said, "Horatio, I know it is none of my business."

"Never mind that, sir," Father said. "Say what you wish."

"Don't do it," Philip said. "If you just clean the paint off and say nothing, they might paint the monument again, but they will get tired of painting and then everything will be the same and people here will go back to remembering General Adams as a hero. But if you move him, then the story will never die. Everybody will be so busy remembering that the stone was painted and that you moved the grave because it was painted, they will forget about the war and about the battle. They will just keep on handing down the story of the painted stone."

"They will remember that I loved him enough to protect him," Father said, "won't they?"

"They will remember that you moved the grave," Philip said.

"Yes," Father said quickly, his voice strong. "Yes, by God, they will remember that!"

So it was settled. Father had already made the arrangements. The undertaker was coming up the next morning to have the removal permit signed and to open the grave. Before we went in to dinner, Father invited Philip to remain with us that night and to go with him to the cemetery and, out of his interest in history, or out of simple curiosity, Philip agreed. Father invited the rest of us to go, too, and I decided that if Philip were going I might be able to stand it. Tavean looked at Emily and she turned paler than ever; she took a big sip of martini and said, yes, it would be better to see it all. She would prefer going to the cemetery with Father, to sitting at home and waiting, and being at home, in the house, when the hearse came up the drive. Then Tavean said he believed he could make it on his crutches.

So we all agreed to go together, to be there when the first clods were lifted, and to come, in procession I supposed, back to Adams' Rest for the new burial. After dinner was over, Philip and I drove in to Van Buren to get some cigarettes and, because it was a pretty night, the air cool, but not cold, the moon full, we did not come directly home but drove on back out the highway and parked on a hill and looked at the moonlit country. The ground we looked at was the field of the old battle where my great-grandfather and all those other men had died. There was an historical marker on the hill, a plaque telling where the different corps and divisions had been deployed. We got out of the car and read the marker and stood by the railing and looked down over the valley. Philip pointed out a few of the landmarks; the river and one or two of the houses and the old roadbed. Then I asked him to show me where Grandfather Adams had probably been killed.

"I don't know," he said. "It could have been anywhere."

"Can you look it up?" I asked.

"No," he replied. "There's no way of telling. The report in the *Official Records* simply lists him as being killed at Van Buren. He was not with his regular division. As I told you once, they were not even in the battle. So there's no knowing where he was or what he was doing." Then he put his arm around my waist and looked down at me and smiled and said, "I know I love you. I'm mighty certain of that."

He kissed me, and we stood there for a little while longer. Then we got in the car and went back home.

We went back to the house that had once belonged to my Great-grandfather Adams when he had been alive as Father was now alive, or rather as Philip and I were now alive, because he had not lived to be as old as Father. We drove up to the front porch and got out and went across the porch and in through the hall into the living room. It was not late and I do not believe that anyone in the house was asleep, but the servants had finished in the kitchen and gone, and Emily and Father were upstairs, and Tavean was in his big room behind the library; it was very quiet with only the sound of the fire's draught and the faint rasp of the lighter which Philip held to my cigarette. I sat down on a couch and I thought he would sit down beside me, but he did not. He stood in the middle of the floor, his hands in his pockets, his eyes peering down through his spectacles at the carpet. He looked a little embarrassed, almost a little fearful, and I knew suddenly that he was going to propose to me, and I was glad.

"I love you," he said, speaking rapidly, "and I want you to marry me. Will you marry me, Anne?"

The way he had asked was not very romantic, but hearing him speak the words—no matter how fast or how fearfully—made me very happy, happier even than I had thought they would make me, though I loved him very much. I felt even a bit tearful, as I used to feel when Tavean spoke kindly to me or when Father or Mother gave me a nice present that I did not expect, but more than this, more profoundly moved. I felt a little like weeping, but not for sorrow and not exactly for joy—though I was joyful—but for love, which is like joy and sorrow too, and like all other things you can feel, I suppose, if you love very much and feel the love deeply. I knew that it was time to say yes, and I knew that in a moment I would say yes, but a part of my brain—which was the cautious part, or maybe just the little girl's part, or maybe the part that wanted to remain a spinster—kept saying that I ought to think it over, consider Philip and consider the future with him and how life would be twenty years or thirty years from now if we both lived. But it was very hard to do this, looking at him now; when the short brown hair showed no gray, and the gray eyes showed no dullness, and the flesh on his face was firm, the skin unlined. I could only think that I loved him the way he was now, standing in the middle of the floor with his hands in his trouser pockets, trying to smile and not being very successful, and the poor, weak smile not cynical, not even knowing, just fond and afraid.

I had meant to say, yes, my dear. Yes, my darling. But I found that I could not speak very well, so I simply said, "Yes," very softly and nodded my head.

Then Philip came to sit beside me on the couch.

Later, we decided that we ought to have a drink to celebrate and we went into the dining room and rummaged through the liquor closet, laughing and stopping to kiss, pulling out bottles and reading the labels carefully, as if they meant something or as if it made any difference what we drank.

"Scotch?" Philip said. "Bourbon? Gin? Brandy?"

"Brandy," I replied. "Oh, let's drink brandy."

"Courvoisier?" he said, setting out a dark bottle, "or Remy Martin?"

"Darling," I asked, "which is the best?"

And he said, "How in the hell would a college professor know?"

So we took both bottles and four glasses and we went back into the living room and filled two of the glasses with Courvoisier and the other two with Remy Martin, not because we wanted to know which was better, or even because we thought our palates were good enough to tell, but because we wanted to drink the best in the house, and no mistake about this, because we were going to be married and that was something to celebrate.

I guess we drank a lot of brandy, sitting together very close with the brandy glasses in no sort of order on the table, neither of us knowing which kind we were drinking, and both of us drinking out of the same glass most of the time. We would take a sip and kiss, and then kiss once more before we drank again. I remember that once I looked away from Philip, cast my glance around the living room, and the room looked very warm and soft. The light came dimly, softly from the lamp near the door, and beyond the hearth, the fire was burning out, with the logs glowing red and turning to ash and a warm blue flame burning, flickering close among the embers. The blue flame was barely visible and the hearth was in shadows and, above the mantel, Great-grandfather Adams' portrait was in shadows, too, so I did not worry about him; I turned back to Philip. I turned back to his touch, to the weight and stroke of his hand on my flesh, to his lips that were soft against mine, and very warm and sweet from the brandy.

Finally, he took another drink and I took another drink, and he said, "Do you know what I think? I think you'll probably be a very funny little old lady. Pretty, of course, but very funny."

"Funny-looking," I said. "I'm a funny-looking, little young lady."

"Darling, darling," he said, speaking very softly, his breath and his words very close to my ear, "you are beautiful."

This was a lie, of course, but I did not argue. For this night, at least, I tried to believe him.

So I said, "When I get old, I will probably be fat."

"I couldn't care less," he replied. "I love you. And I will always love you. Get old, and we will get old and fat together, and it will be good living all those years together and good being old and I will love you."

"Oh, my dear," I said, "I will love you, too."

We sat there for a long time, making plans and deciding nothing. We talked of where we would live when we were married, and where we would go on our honeymoon, and what we would have for breakfast in the mornings and for dinner at night. But we did not even set a date for the wedding; I needed a little time to think about that. After a while, we said good night and went to bed.

During the night it rained, and the next day the ground was damp, the air was raw and cold, and the sky was cloudy. For the first time since we had been at Adams' Rest, we all had breakfast together, Emily and Father and

Tavean and I and, of course, Philip. I remember that when Emily came into the dining room she looked, if possible, paler than she had looked the night before. I think there had been some question in all our minds about how we should dress for this occasion, whether we should consider it a kind of funeral or just an excursion on a nasty, wet day, and Emily had hit upon a kind of compromise. She wore a very plainly-tailored gray suit and medium heeled pumps that were going to sink into the cemetery mud, and she had brought downstairs with her, a long gray leather coat with a leather hat to go with it. Father was dressed somewhat formally. He wore a dark brown business suit, a starched white shirt, a black tie. Philip was dressed in the suit he had worn the night before. I wore a skirt. Tavean had on slacks and a long-sleeved woolen sport shirt.

Dressed as we were, we did not seem to fit together and, at the table, when we sat down to breakfast, we behaved almost as strangers, so little could any of us think of to say.

"It's a bad morning," Philip said, but he did not sound like he really thought it was a bad morning. His voice was gay. He looked at me and smiled and I smiled back.

"Yes," Father said seriously. "It rained last night. I regret the rain."

"It will make the ground soft for the diggers," Tavean said.

Nobody replied to this. Father looked grim and a little disgruntled.

"I mean," Tavean said, "it's an ill wind that blows no good."

"We understood that," Father replied. "Let's go to the cemetery."

There were only five of us, but we went in two automobiles. Tavean said he wanted to try out his new car and to test his own ability to drive it, so it appeared that when we came back to Adams' Rest, we would be a small procession after all. Father and Emily, Philip and I got in Father's black De Soto. Tavean trailed us in his pale blue Thunderbird, around the statue that still wore its red and blue paint and which did indeed look like an Indian on the warpath, and out the highway to the gates of the cemetery and down the drive and around the long curve to Great-grandfather Adams' monument and on past this a little way to leave room for the hearse. We got out and Philip helped Tavean get himself and his cast out of the Thunderbird. In a silence heavier than that of the breakfast table, we waited for Mr. Rathbone to arrive.

There was a slight mist falling and a slight wind blowing, not constantly, but in gusts that were very cold. The ground was soggy and the gray stones were wet and dark against the dark skyline and the trees were bare and black and dripping water. On Great-grandfather Adams' grave, that space of earth in front of his marker, the brown grass was matted in dampness, and the little Confederate flag hung limp and faded and wet. We stood with dour faces and thought our dour thoughts, Emily pale and Father determined and Philip trying to hide his morning joy and looking lugubrious. Tavean leaned on his crutches and swung his cast.

Finally, the black hearse turned in at the gate and behind it came Mr. McMurtry's yellow police car. The hearse stopped and Mr. McMurtry, who was alone in the car, stopped behind it. Then the driver of the hearse motioned for Mr. McMurtry to back up, and Mr. McMurtry did, and the hearse turned around to get the back doors as close as possible to Great-grandfather Adams' burying place. Two Negro men got out of the back of the hearse carrying picks and shovels, and Mr. Rathbone and another white man got out of the front, and then took from the back a long canvas bag and a stretcher. Mr. McMurtry left his car and came to Father.

"Mr. Adams," Mr. McMurtry said, "you can't do this. It won't do at all to be tampering with the cemetery."

Father looked at Mr. Rathbone. "Did you get the permit signed?"

Mr. Rathbone was a portly man, short, with short fat legs and a round stomach. He was wearing a trench coat buttoned up at his neck and a felt hat, which he had removed and replaced quickly when he spoke to Emily and me. Between the hat and the collar you could see only his wide nose, his full lips, his rosy cheeks, and his quick, bright, brown eyes which were set close together.

"Yes, sir," Mr. Rathbone said, "I have it, Mr. Adams."

"Then show it to Mr. McMurtry, please," Father nodded his head at Mr. McMurtry.

But Mr. McMurtry waved the paper away.

"I know about that, Mr. Adams," he said. "I was there when this gentleman come in to have it signed. That's why I drove out here to appeal to you. To ask you not to do this."

"Then you have wasted your time," Father said. "I'm going to take my grandfather home where he will be safe from vandals."

Mr. McMurtry stood very straight and looked at Father and bit his lip. "Mr. Adams," he said, "the dead is sacred."

"Indeed they are, sir," Father said. "That's why I intend to open this grave. There are some people around here who apparently don't agree with us."

It was about then, I think, that the first of the cars began to arrive. Mr. Rathbone had worked efficiently. He had got the permit signed and come directly to the cemetery from the courthouse. He had done his best. But he and Father, both being city men, had not realized how quickly information could spread in a small town, a village. First came an old Ford with two young men in it, boys eighteen or twenty years old, who had probably abandoned high school and not yet gone to work. One of them wore a raincoat, the other a leather jacket and Levi's. They parked their car and walked up to stand beside the gravestone.

"What do you want?" Father said to them angrily.

"Nothing," the boy in the leather jacket replied impudently. "It's public property, ain't it? We just aim to stand here."

But by this time, the second car had come and after it came the third and, for sure, we did have a real funeral procession now, or it would be a procession if we all started our automobiles and got moving. The crowd that gathered were men mostly, and this seemed right. Opening a grave after almost a hundred years was not the sort of spectacle that was likely to appeal to women. It appeared that not only every loafer in town had come out but that some of the businessmen had come, too. It was as if only the clerks and secretaries had been left behind to answer the phones and keep the stores.

"Oh," Emily said, "look at them. There are so many, Horatio."

"I don't care," Father said. "I have the signed permit. They cannot stop me."

We stood in the middle of the crowd; men in suits, men in over-alls, but there were a few women. One of them was an old lady whom I recognized as Mrs. Ashley, who was a Confederate grandchild herself, but not the granddaughter of a general. Mrs. Ashley was a good deal older than Father. She was too old to be out in the December weather and she did not have the clothes for this sort of excursion. She came up to Father in a black cloth coat, a plain black hat on her gray old head, dressed as women dress when they get old enough whether they are rich or poor, kind or irascible. She took off her glasses and wiped them clear and put them back on and looked at Father and said, "Mr. Adams, Mr. Adams. Oh, sir, what do you mean?"

"Mrs. Ashley," Father replied gently, "you know what has happened. I have been driven to this. I do not want to do it."

"Then don't do it!" Mrs. Ashley said sharply. "You must not do it! You must leave General Adams here with the other soldiers!"

"Look," Father said, his voice still gentle, but a little more urgent. He pointed to the painted headstone.

"I know," she replied. "I have seen it. It hurts me, too."

"Then you understand," Father told her. "You see why I'm going to take my grandfather back home."

"No, no!" Mrs. Ashley said. Then she turned to the crowd which had been listening in silence; the frail little woman turned carefully, moved her feet with care on the soft ground, and said in an old, frail voice, "Oh, good people, don't let him do this. Help me. Help me to make him see he is wrong."

I thought for a moment that she had stopped him. I believe that she would have stopped him if it had not been for the two boys who had been the first of the crowd—one in a raincoat, the other in a leather jacket. When Mrs. Ashley stopped speaking, Father did not say anything and Mr. McMurtry did not say anything, and a man I did not know came up to Father and called him Horatio and asked him not to open the grave. He told Father that the town at large was not guilty. He said that only a few people in the town were guilty and that what Father was about to do would hurt the town. I do not know what he had in his mind. He was thinking maybe of how the battlefield and the cemetery were—in a limited sense at least—a tourist attraction. Maybe he was from the Chamber of Commerce or maybe not. Maybe he was like Mrs. Ashley and revered the past.

At any rate, Father hesitated. He looked around at the crowd of people, many of whom were his friends. He looked at Emily's pale face and at me and at Tavean and at Philip, and he knew what we all thought. He looked down at his feet for a while, then once more raised his eyes. "I don't know," he said. "Mr. McMurtry doesn't seem to be able to find the vandals. He can't find out who it is that keeps painting this stone."

And the boy in the leather jacket laughed. At the mention of Mr. McMurtry's incompetence, he guffawed, and the boy in the raincoat smiled. I do not know whether they were the vandals who had painted the stones, for they would not likely be in sympathy with Mr. McMurtry in any event. But I know that Father thought they were the vandals, and whether they were or not, obviously they approved of the vandalism. Father looked at the two boys and his face grew red. Then he turned to Mr. Rathbone and said, "Go ahead. Let's do what we came for."

So with the crowd still around us, watching, the two Negroes began to dig in the wet ground. In the space in front of the headstone, they marked off the limits of the grave and for a few moments they went at their work lustily. They went down quickly to a depth of three or four feet and then they began to work carefully and mostly with their shovels. Mr. Rathbone directed them in quiet but plainly audible tones. He told them that there would be no casket, that if there had ever been one, it would have rotted away. He cautioned them to work a little earth at a time and to be on the lookout for the first sign of the body. He himself stood at the edge of the grave and stared intently into it.

The Negroes continued to dig. The earth piled up. Soon we could not see anything of the hole or of the Negroes, and I was glad of this, for I did not want to see, but I could not stop watching. We stood and listened to the soft fall of the pick in the soft wet earth, the soft chunk and scrape of the shovel. Finally, the other white man who had come with Mr. Rathbone left the stretcher and the canvas bag and went to stand beside Mr. Rathbone and peer down into the grave with him. They spoke in whispers to each other.

Mr. Rathbone came to speak to Father, and I was standing beside Father, and I heard Mr. Rathbone say, "We are down six feet already and we haven't found him."

"What do you mean?" Father said.

"We haven't come on the body yet," Mr. Rathbone replied, his voice still low. "Are you sure we are digging in the right place? Are you certain he's not on the other side of the headstone?"

"Of course, I'm sure," Father said crossly. "This has always been his grave. This is where we have always put the flowers."

He glanced at Philip. "They must have buried them deeper then. Isn't that so, Philip?"

Philip hesitated, then shook his head. "No, sir, shallower, if anything. They didn't have much time to dig, with a war going on."

"Keep digging," Father said.

And they did keep digging and the crowd began to murmur. The crowd talked and speculated and the hole got deeper. Finally the grave was eight feet deep and still there was no body.

"It's no use," Mr. Rathbone said. "We're digging in the wrong place. If he had been buried there, we would have found him."

"Then where is he?" Father said desperately.

"I don't know," Mr. Rathbone said. "I thought maybe he would be behind the marker, but there is somebody else buried there. There is not room between General Adams' marker and the next headstone."

"Then we have gone to the side of him," Father said. "He is a little to the right or to the left."

But Father was looking at the stones, the arrangement of the graves, and undoubtedly he could tell, as we could tell, that if Great-grandfather were buried here at all we would have discovered him.

"We will find him to one side," Father said, but his voice was very weak and without conviction.

And, of course, we did not find him. The gravediggers dug a while longer. Then they filled up their hole and we all left the cemetery and went back home.

7

The Life and Times of Horatio Adams

On that morning in December, I stood and looked into the empty grave and it took me a little while to convince myself that the grave was empty. I suppose when you have believed something all your life you cannot stop believing it, no matter how obvious it is that you have been wrong, no matter how irrefutable the evidence. I had told Mr. Rathbone to enlarge the hole, to dig deeper and wider until he had found the body. He had dug on and found nothing and there was no place around the marker left to dig.

"Where is he?" I asked Rathbone.

And Rathbone had said, "I don't know."

Then I said, "Look at all these people. Look at this crowd staring and gaping at us. I told you not to let anybody know what we were going to do."

He regarded me for a moment in silence. His eyes narrowed, but for the most part, his face remained calm. Finally he said, "I didn't tell anybody. I had to get the permit signed, Mr. Adams. You knew about that."

I did not reply. For it was over now, the anger had passed. I felt too weak to be mad, even at the two vandals who were staring with interest into the empty grave. For a moment, I felt nothing. I turned back toward the car and Emily and Anne and Philip came with me. I got in and started the engine and drove slowly out the drive. I passed through the gate and moved down the highway, seeing very clearly the road in front of me; the white line, and the black, wet asphalt, and seeing, too, the land on each side; the brown fields and the first houses as we came toward town. I remember saying to myself, *He was not there.* And then saying to myself, as I had said to Rathbone, *Where is he?*

And the disappointment started, which was like heartbreak, which was like death or the irretrievable loss of love. I endured it as best I could and kept my gaze on the road and did not look at Emily. We passed the statue of the Confederate soldier, still painted, his face still striped like that of an Indian, and swung around the sq are and were out on the highway again, and at last I felt that I might trust myself to speak.

"Philip," I said, "where is he? We have got to find him."

"I don't know where he is," Philip replied. "I don't have any idea."

"God damn it!" I said, "he is somewhere and you have got to help me find him. I've got to have him back home at Adams' Rest."

I know they did not understand it. We rode along in the car and all of them—Emily and Anne and Philip—thought me a fool to be so much exercised over the body of a man who had been dead for nearly a hundred years.

And I knew now that there was no use trying to explain it. I might have said to them, *But don't you see? It has something to do with all of us. What I want to find is something that we all can be proud of, something that will stand with us against the steady course of time and the forgetfulness of man.* I could have said this. And I could have said, *You cannot live forever. You have got to die, as he had to die, and that being so, all you can hope for out of life is to be remembered.* But which of them would have understood that, basking now as they did in their warm and youthful blood, seeing as they did the years of their lives laid long before them?

I think at that moment that I almost hated them for being young, but I did not envy them. I did not wish to be young like them. I only wished that they could understand, could know what I felt, and share my anguish and I wished to God they knew how to help me find my grandfather's body.

"Philip," I said again, "you have got to help me."

And he replied, "I will. I will do all I can."

When we got home, Philip and Anne remained downstairs and I went up to the bedroom with Emily. I remember watching her as she climbed the steps before me—the gentle swing of her gray leather coat, the movement of the black shoes soiled by the cemetery mud, the little spot of mud that had splashed up on her ankle. I saw her smooth, youthful legs without really seeing them, without thinking of what it was I saw, just as I noticed the stripe in the wallpaper and the crystal glow of the bracket lamps when we had reached the upper hallway.

Inside the bedroom, Emily took off her coat and hat and threw them on a chair, and I saw this, too, without noticing, without considering how unusual this was for her, for Emily was the soul of neatness. I went to the window, to stand there and look out. From the window I could see the cemetery, our own private little graveyard where I had meant to bring Grandfather Adams. This did register on my brain and I thought I was going to cry, but I controlled myself. I got a grip on my emotions and I stayed there and looked at the family cemetery and thought about all the things that had happened that day, and about how little of what had happened had been what I had expected. I thought of the crowd which should not have been there and particularly of those two boys who had been rude to me and who had laughed at me and at McMurtry. And I thought of the empty grave which was not a grave but was just a big, deep, muddy hole, and I clamped my teeth together and tried to stop thinking.

But sometimes when your mind starts working, you cannot make it stop and the more you try to make it stop, the more you keep on thinking and that is the way it was with me that day. I went on remembering. I recalled how when I was a little boy I had come to stand beside Grandfather Adams' grave and be proud of him. I saw in my mind's eye the image of the child who had been myself, and I was dressed in the foolish clothes of 1915. I stood in a belted tweed coat, a matching cap, a mourning band around my arm for my dead mother and father. It was spring; the grass on the grave was green and there were fresh flowers in a vase and a flag near the marker. Then the image changed and the little boy was still there, but it was fall and the grave was open as it had been open this morning and it was empty. This was a silly thing for a man to think. It was like a dream, but I thought it for a moment at least. Then I was conscious of Emily standing beside me.

She was pale but I was about to get used to that. She had been pale since the night before, when I had told her that I intended to move Grandfather's body. I had come back from Nashville with my plan already made and I was very happy that I was going to be avenged on the town for the vandalism it had allowed, and happy with the thought that my grandfather's stone would be secure and that his body would be near me now, and that when I died I would be buried near him. I felt, I suppose, like a man feels when something very good has happened to him, when he has been promoted in his firm, or when he has made a profitable deal, or won a big case, or successfully performed a difficult operation. But what I felt was more even than this. It was a sense of adventure. It was what the general must feel when he has his flanks secure and his artillery in place and he looks down the valley to see the enemy coming closer. It was what men used to feel when they grounded the boats and moved up on the strange and glittering beach and glimpsed in the distance, the heavy growth of the fecund jungle. Or maybe it was not this either. Maybe what I felt was just what the selfish boy feels when he has won all the marbles. However this was, on my way home that day I whistled along with the radio, I gripped the steering wheel hard from time to time. From time to time, I felt a thrill in my breast and bowels.

But Emily had not been thrilled. When I had told her

what I intended to do, the color had drained from her cheeks and there had been tight little lines in her face, around her eyes and mouth and across her forehead. She had said nothing.

Now, standing beside me in the bedroom, she was still very pale. The pale flesh was still taut and she did not speak now, either. She stood and I stood and outside, the rain came down, fell gently on the stones of the family graveyard, fell on the dead lawn and the dead garden.

Finally I looked down at her and said, "I guess you are happy now. I guess you're glad you didn't have to look at a skeleton."

"Oh, no!" she said and began to cry. "Oh, no! I wish he had been there. Oh, I wish very much that you had found your grandfather!" She crossed the room and sat down and put her face in her hands. I could hear her sobbing. I could see her body tremble with the sobs and I was sorry for the way that I had spoken to her. I went to her and put my hand on her shoulder.

"My dear," I said, "that was wrong. I did not mean to say that."

She did not look up. Speaking in a muffled, tearful voice, she said, "It's all right. I'm going to be all right. Just give me a minute."

I removed my hand from her shoulder. I took off my coat and loosened my tie and lay down on the counterpane. I stayed there looking up at the gathered, folded silk of the tester, and the sobs softened and stopped at last. There was only Emily's loud and irregular breathing. Then this, too, was past and she left her chair, but she kept her face turned away from me.

"I'll be all right," she said again in a tight, trembling voice. "It's just that I got a little cold at the cemetery. Let me take a shower."

She picked up her coat and hat and went into the dressing room. I listened to Emily's movements without really hearing them, just as, earlier that morning, I had looked at the world without quite seeing it. Once or twice she opened the closet door. Then she was in the bathroom and there was the sound of the toilet flushing and later the noise of water running in the shower. Then there was movement in the dressing room once again.

While Emily was bathing, I was thinking of what the next step would be in the search for my grandfather. I would have to consult with Philip. It seemed to me that we might start with a collection of Grandfather Adams' papers that were preserved in a cabinet in the library. There were some letters he had written home from the war, a diary he had kept. These, I thought, might lead us to other papers—letters, journals, narratives—that might shed some light on the whereabouts of his body.

After a while the door to the dressing room opened and Emily came into the bedroom.

I had, of course, expected her to change her clothes. She had gotten damp at the cemetery and I would not have been surprised to see her come out in a fresh dress and different shoes, or in a skirt with perhaps a sweater thrown over her shoulders. But she came out in a robe and slippers and she moved slowly, laboriously, as if she were walking in deep sand, or as if the air itself resisted her step like water. She came to the edge of the bed and in a strained voice that echoed her recent tears, she said. "Get up. Get up, Horatio and let me turn down the cover."

Preoccupied as I was—or maybe just dense as I am—I thought only that she was tired and wanted to rest, and the idea that she was going to take a nap before lunch annoyed me a little. After her weeping, it was somehow like the old fashion of a woman taking to her bed against the stresses and strains of life, the griefs of existence. I grunted and rose and took a step or two into the room. Then I turned around to see the cover pulled back and to see Emily slip out of her robe and stand by the bed, naked.

She stood for a moment facing me with her hands at her sides. Then she lowered her naked hips to the bed, pulled up her long, naked thighs, and gracefully thrust her legs beneath the sheet. "Come on," she said. "Come on, now. I am ready."

In my surprise—or more than that, my shock—I made no move and no reply. I waited in the middle of the floor in stunned silence. I did not want to make love to Emily—not at this moment anyway—and I had not dreamed that she wanted me to make love to her and then it struck me that she did not want me to. I did not know yet why she had taken off her clothes and come out of the dressing room and got in bed and offered herself to me. But it was obvious from her face, which remained pale and drawn, that she anticipated no joy in our coming together, that she looked for no pleasure in the warm and fleshly contact. Beneath the cover, her body lay rigid; stiffly on the pillow lay her head. The tearstains had been washed off her face in the shower, but her eyes remained red and a little swollen. She lifted one hand out from under the counterpane, rubbed it across her forehead, then lowered it again.

"Emily," I said coldly, "this is not necessary."

"Come on," she said, her voice barely under control. "At least let me do this much. Oh, at least let me be this much to you."

Now it did come to me, not what she had expected of me—any idiot would have known that—but why she expected it. Suddenly, I remembered another time when death and my dead grandfather had been much on our minds. On the day after the first act of vandalism, I had tried to explain to Emily why I was so deeply moved by the painting of the headstone. I had told her how much I loved her and how much I would hate to be parted from her and how certain it was that both of us were going to die. Then I had guided her to the bed and coldly, and against her desire, I had lain down with her.

I remembered from the days when I used to read books, that an Englishman who lived a long time ago, a man named Locke, had had a theory about the human memory. He had spoken of it as the association of ideas, and the way it worked was that if you once got two ideas associated in your mind, you never thought of one without thinking of the other. So I guess if you were Eve, every time you saw an apple you thought of the serpent, and if you were Emily Adams, every time your husband spoke of death you thought of taking off your clothes and getting in bed, no matter how you felt or whether the mood were upon you. And I knew that this association of Emily's was not such an original one after all. I thought of this, being a man and having a man's futile urge to categorize the world, to explain away the world's guilt in an oversimplification.

But this was not all I thought. I recollected that other day when I had spoken of death and then made love to Emily, and then something happened that Locke did not explain—or maybe he did explain and I was too obtuse to understand it. Remembering that other act of love, which had been coldly, almost cruelly performed, I felt a sudden and strong desire and I knew that I would take her. That time when I had taken her first against her will seemed suddenly sweeter to me than all the other times, more tempting than the moments of our honeymoon and all tempting moments afterward. In my imagination I felt again the stiffness of her thighs, the awkwardness of the unwilling hips, the body rigid beneath mine, as it lay rigid on the bed now beneath the cover.

"Come on," she said and I went to her very quickly.

Hurriedly, I removed my clothes and got in bed and took her in my arms and, soon after we had begun to make love, Emily once again started crying. I was conscious of her sobs against the rhythm of our movement, conscious of her tears cold on my own cheek. But I did not stop. I did not hesitate. When we had finished she continued to weep for a while. Then she said, "Oh, I had hoped you would find your grandfather and bring him back here. I had hoped that when you had buried him here, we would be done with death forever."

I lay in bed with Emily for a little while. Then I got up and put on my clothes and went downstairs. I was looking for Philip and I found him in the living room, sitting on a couch with Anne, his arm around her shoulder; there was lipstick on his mouth. He got up rather hurriedly when he saw me standing in the doorway.

"Excuse me," I said. "I'm afraid I have intruded on you."

"No, sir," Philip said. "As a matter of fact I wanted to see you. That is I wanted to ask you . . . speak to you. . . ." And his voice trailed off.

Anne said, "We are going to be married, Father. Philip asked me to marry him and I told him yes."

I said nothing.

"He is going to be your son-in-law," Anne said. "Aren't you glad?"

"Yes," I said weakly. "Yes, indeed."

And I suppose I was glad, happy that she was going to marry, and content that she was going to marry Philip; and I guess I had known that she loved him and that he loved her, and the announcement should have come to me as no surprise. But it was a surprise because Anne was my little girl and I could not quite think of her as being married. All her life she had been my daughter, and all the other things she had been were secondary to that. She had been my daughter who was a schoolgirl, or my daughter who was a member of a certain sorority, or my daughter who worked for the Red Cross, or took a trip, or went to the hairdresser. Even when she had gone out with boys, to dances or to movies, or later to cocktail parties, she had been my daughter who was out on a date; or going down the aisle at the church, she had been my daughter who also happened to be the bridesmaid. Now, she would be Mrs. Philip Holcomb, the wife of an assistant professor of history, and only incidentally now Horatio Adams' daughter.

I looked at her and at Philip. She sat with her feet together on the floor, her skirt pulled smoothly down over her knees, but her lipstick was smeared and her blouse was wrinkled and her hair was slightly disarrayed. Philip stood near her with his mouth red, his face flushed, his glasses sliding a little forward on the bridge of his nose. I regarded them and they gazed at each other, stared foolishly and romantically into each other's eyes like two of nature's innocent and unsullied children. And that is what they were or seemed to me to be—children—and I was the oldest man on the face of the earth. I could not imagine them being married. When I tried to think of it, I kept seeing a little boy and a little girl eternally playing house.

But it occurred to me that there was nothing that I could do to keep them from getting married, and it occurred to me, too, that this little boy who was going to wed my daughter was the same little boy who was going to help me find my grandfather's bones. I congratulated them. I shook Philip's hand and kissed Anne's cheek, and I told Philip that I would like to talk to him sometime. There were some things I wanted to show him. Then I left the living room and crossed the hall and went into the library. I thought I would unlock the cabinet and get out grandfather's letters and journals, but they were already spread out on the library table. Tavean was reading them by the light of a lamp.

I went in and sat down opposite him, took my place on the other side of that table which was strewn with loose sheets of old and foxing paper, with pocket-sized books with cracked bindings. The clue that I was searching for was written here somewhere, knowledge was recorded here in fading brown or black or purple ink.

"I'm surprised," I said to Tavean. "I didn't expect to find you reading all this. I didn't know you were interested."

He smiled. He was a very charming boy. When he smiled, his lips parted to show very even, white teeth, and there were little wrinkles of joy around his eyes.

"Well," he replied, "maybe I'm not interested, at least not like you are."

"Tell me about it," I said, waving my hand toward the scattered papers. "Tell me why you are doing this."

He smiled once more. "It's a mystery," he said. "I mean when you go there and see that the body is not where you thought it was, you wonder where it is. It's like losing anything else, I guess, only this is even stranger and more intriguing because it is a body that is missing. You want to find the body and solve the mystery."

"And of course," I said ironically, "this body happens to be that of your great-grandfather. That might add to the mystery, too."

"Yes," he agreed. "It's Grandfather Adams' body. That's right."

"And that's all you think?" I said. "That's the only reason you have for straining your eyes on that dim writing?"

"Yes," he said pleasantly, "I guess so."

"Well," I said, "you have an admirable curiosity. But maybe if you keep on reading those letters, it will occur to you that we weren't exactly on a scavenger hunt this morning. This is a little more than a mystery for us to amuse ourselves with."

I got up and walked to the mantel, picked up a silver snuff box that was sitting there, looked at the engraving on the top, and set the box gently down. Then I said, "Tavean, you're like everybody else in this house. You're a damned fool!"

Tavean did not reply immediately. He took out his cigarettes, drew one carefully from the package, flicked his lighter, and blew smoke at the lamp. He watched the gray smoke rise. He looked at it as it curled under the lampshade, thinned out, and rose toward the ceiling. Then he puffed his cigarette again.

"All right," he said finally, "I'm a fool. But I'm a live fool and Great-grandfather Adams is dead. And I don't mean to let a dead hero ruin a live fool's life."

"You don't understand," I said sharply. "You're alive, yes, and the trouble is you think you are going to stay alive. You think you're going to live forever!"

"No, I don't," Tavean said, "or maybe I do. But that's not the point. That's not what I'm talking about. What I do think is that when I'm dead I won't know much then. I won't give a damn one way or the other what anybody does with the carcass."

"It's not that simple," I said. "It's not just a matter of what the dead man wants. One man dies, but he leaves others. There are always the living."

"Then consider the living," Tavean said. "Think of some of the living besides yourself. Think of Anne. Think of Emily."

He dropped Emily's name between us in a tone of great concern, almost of anguish. He spoke the name of my wife as if she were the thing that he cherished most among all the things and people in the world. I had remained standing by the mantel, and to look at me he had to turn half around in his chair; his face was away from the lamp, his features were indistinct in the room's shadows. Suddenly, it came to me what I had known for a long time, I suppose, but what, in my concern for my grandfather, I had tried to put temporarily out of my mind, I had almost forgotten. He was in love with Emily and there was a good chance that she loved him, too. She had wept over his accident. She had gone to visit him when he lay asleep in the clinic. During the days when he had lain in bed, Emily had kept him company while I was in town, Emily had sat with him and talked with him and—but I could not go beyond this. I could not yet let myself think of what might have happened.

Nor could I answer him at once.

For a moment, it seemed to me that the main concern of my life was to maintain my composure, to make no move, to give no sign that would show him what I felt; the grief and the sudden fear that lay beneath my anger. I stood very still, facing Tavean for as long as I could. Then I made myself go toward him. I walked slowly toward the table where he was sitting. Slowly I lowered myself into a chair. I faced Tavean once more, looked at him once more in the bright lamplight that shone on the old letters, the old diaries.

"Would you do this to me?" I said. "Would you court my wife in my own house? Would you try to take her from me?"

"No," he said, "not like that. I would not. But look at yourself. Look what you are doing to her."

"Yes," I replied, "that's the way we do things now, isn't it? Whatever a man does these days, it's not his fault, it's somebody else's. Every murderer who gets brought to trial sits up on the witness stand and says he did it, but it wasn't really his fault, something or somebody else made him do it. Well, whatever you and Emily do, whatever you have done is not done because of me. You do simply what you want to do and I can understand your desires. I can see through them. I am not blind. And I am not so old either as you apparently think I am."

"Take her back to Nashville," Tavean said. "Get her away from here. Give these papers to Philip and let him find your body for you. But don't make Emily watch while he looks for it. And don't make her listen to you talk about it every minute of the day."

"Take her to Nashville," I said scornfully. "Yes. You advised me to do that once before. And you said something else. You said you were going to take yourself back there. But you didn't do it."

"No," he replied, "I did not go. I stayed because you decided to dig up Great-grandfather's body, because you were going to make her submit to the opening of the grave."

That was the word he used—submit. As if the moving of the corpse would somehow be a violation of Emily, a vile attack on her person, a tawdry compromise of her honor.

"And that's why you stayed?"

"Yes," he said, "that's the reason."

"Tavean," I said, "I ought not to put up with this. I ought to throw you out of this house. I ought to make you leave. But, God help me, I cannot do that anymore than I can forget about your great-grandfather and let him stay buried wherever he is, in whatever unknown grave. It is all part of the same thing, but you don't understand it."

I got up then and left the room.

Tavean would not join us for lunch and Emily would not come down from her room, so there were only three of us in the dining room; Anne, Philip, and I. Except that I do not think that Anne and Philip knew there were three of us. I think, for most of the meal, they were conscious only of themselves. They sat and looked at each other and laughed frequently about things that did not strike me as being amusing. Then, suddenly, one of them would recollect my presence and rather sheepishly address a remark to me. I hated to spoil their tender moment, but I needed Philip's help and I could not wait until he offered it.

After luncheon, I insisted that he go to the library with me, and I stayed there with him while he read the letters and sorted them out and looked over the journals. He seemed to be very efficient, almost coldly so. He read with haste and with no change of expression. He would pick up a paper and peer at it intently for a moment, put it aside and pick up another paper as if he were grading student examinations or looking over letters that had been written yesterday or the day before. He seemed to have no concept of the man who had written the letters or of the war they had come out of or of the suffering that the war had made the man endure. He smoked and read and said nothing. In silence, I waited and fidgeted in my chair.

Finally, he looked up and took off his spectacles and rubbed his eyes.

"Can you find him?" I asked.

"I don't know," he said, "we don't have much to go on. I'd say the chances of finding him were pretty slim."

"You've got to find him," I said.

He shrugged slightly. "I'll do my best."

"Listen," I said, "he was a man, don't you know that? Those are letters you were reading, not a story in a book."

I had seen the papers many times, and I remembered a passage from a letter that my grandfather had written very late in the war to a cousin of his named Obadiah Adams, who lived in south Georgia. Grandfather had apparently seen Obadiah Adams after the Battle of Atlanta. They had perhaps talked about the chances for Southern victory, and for the success of General Hood's Tennessee campaign. At any rate, on the way north with Hood, Grandfather had written Obadiah Adams a touching letter, and I found that letter now and read the last part of it aloud to Philip.

> It is a lonely pursuit to be a member of an army, though it may seem to you curious that one could complain of loneliness surrounded as he be by a score of thousand men. In Tennessee are my youngest child and the grave of my wife, neither of which have I ever seen, nor have I any guarantee or surety now that I shall ever see them. But I should like to live to see them, and I should like to remain on this earth long enough to resume some measure of the soft and sweet existence that was mine to live before this war commenced. I know that win or lose, our world will have changed. I know that the old days are gone as the blessed

face and figure of my wife are gone, and the old comfort. But I should like once more to sit in a chair, to gaze at a fire that is built on dogs, to hear the voice and feel the touch of a genteel woman. May God grant us our victory and our joy!

I stopped reading. "Doesn't that mean anything to you?" I asked. "Don't you see now why I have to bring him home?"

"Of course that means something to me," he replied. "Horatio, I know all about their suffering. At least, I know as much as you can learn about it from reading books. And I have felt it, too, maybe not like you feel it, but enough. Sometimes when you eat, you think about how hungry they were, and sometimes in the winter, when you are out at night and shivering maybe, you think about how cold they were, and you are sorry for them. You are sorry, no matter what your politics or what you feel concerning the things they were fighting for, and you admire them because they were very brave. But then you remember that they are all dead and you cannot share your food with them or give them your coat. And they were not fighting a war just to gain your sympathy and admiration."

He stopped and smiled apologetically. "I talk too much. The point is that there is nothing in that letter to help us find him."

"How will we find him?" I asked.

"Well," he replied, "I can tell you how we'll go about it."

We knew, Philip pointed out, from the letters and the journals, that my grandfather had come north with Hood in 1864, in the campaign that culminated in the Battle of Nashville. We knew that on November 26, he had camped with the army just south of Columbia, Tennessee, and there we lost him. From the time that he had made his last entry in his journal until the report of his death in the *Official Records,* we did not know where he had been.

"Now," Philip said cruelly, "we know that he died and therefore we can expect no more help from him. To find out about the dead, you have to go to somebody who was still living, and that is what we'll try to do. We'll have to get the old regimental rolls—if they still exist—and try to figure out who might have known him and see if some of these people left any documents that will give us a hint as to where he is."

"How long will all this take?"

"Horatio," he said, "success or failure, the length of time involved—from here on it is all purely luck."

"Yes," I said, "all right. But can you do all this in Nashville? In the state archives?"

"I doubt it," he said. "Confederate papers are scattered from here to hell. But don't worry," he added gloomily, "I've got a vacation coming up."

"I'll go with you," I said. "I'll help you."

He shook his head. "No. You hold the fort. But remember, don't get your hopes up. Don't expect too much."

Philip left then. He said good-by to Anne and started to Nashville. I went upstairs to talk to Emily.

I had gone to the bedroom at lunchtime to see whether or not she would come down and eat with us, and she had refused. She had been up and dressed and in complete control of herself, but her eyes were still red, and she did not want anyone to know that she had been crying. She had allowed the maid to bring her some coffee and some soup.

Now, she was seated by a table, reading. She was wearing a tan wool dress with a full skirt and short sleeves and a plain neckline. Her hair was newly combed, her makeup was fresh, and her eyes gave no evidence of her recent tears: her face showed no sorrow. Sitting with her legs crossed, her hands on the magazine, a cigarette smoking in an ashtray, she seemed as completely composed as I had ever seen her. It was as if her day had held no vicissitudes, no uncertainties.

She looked up and in a perfectly normal voice she said, "Hello, Horatio," and then she resumed her reading.

I spoke to her, went in and took a shower, dried myself, and dressed quickly, and came back into the bedroom to knot my tie.

"Emily," I said, "Philip is going to start looking for Grandfather tomorrow. He tells me not to get my hopes up, but I think Philip will find him. I believe we will have him back pretty soon."

"That's nice," she said, "I hope you do."

"Yes," I said, "I'm going to have the stone brought on out here. I want to be ready when Philip tells me where he is."

"I would do that," she said. "Whether Philip finds him or not, it would be kind of awkward to leave the stone where it is."

I looked at her sharply. I had never seen her act this way before. Never before when we had spoken of my dead grandfather had she been the least bit ironic or half so calm. I peered at her but her face showed nothing. Once more she had turned her eyes to her magazine.

"My dear," I said, "Emily. I know this upsets you. But Philip will find him and we will bring him back here and then it will be over. We will know he is safe here and we will never have to go through all this again."

"Over," she said, calmly, coldly, "finished, just like that and we can forget about it. I hope so. And I hope you get him. He's what you want more than anything else in the world."

I did not know what to say. She gave me few words to argue against. I had little to chide her for, except the perfectly even tone of her voice.

Then she said, "Tell me something, Horatio. Why did your first wife kill herself?"

I was speechless, stunned. I caught my breath sharply and I felt my flesh grow cold. For a moment I saw in my mind the dead face of Nancy. Then I brought the world back into focus and I was looking at Emily and she was looking at me.

"You didn't know her," I said, "and you don't have any right to know anything about her. What did you mean by asking me that? What are you trying to say?"

"Nothing," she said, and she smiled at me. Her lips actually drew back in a proper, but somehow joyless, smile. "I was just thinking. Come on, let's go downstairs. Let's have a drink."

We went down and had our drink with Anne and Tavean. And later, we sat around the dinner table as if nothing had happened, as if Tavean and I had never argued, as if Emily had never known of Nancy's existence in the world. Or almost that way, at least. We were almost normal.

A few nights later, Philip called from Nashville to say he had a clue that might lead him to my grandfather. He warned me once more not to be too hopeful, but regardless of his warning, I could not help believing that we would soon have Grandfather Adams back. It occurred to me that I ought to go on with my plans to bury him in the family cemetery. I could bring the stone here and have it cleaned and it would be in position and waiting for the body.

The next day, after lunch, I drove to Van Buren. I went to see about moving the monument. When I returned, Emily and Tavean were gone.

8

*The Recollections of
Anne Adams*

I DID NOT HEAR them leave; rather, I heard the silence that they left behind them. Or maybe this is wrong, too. I suppose what really happened was that I got bored with myself, tired of sitting in my room thinking of Philip and missing him, and I just went downstairs and saw that Emily and Tavean were no longer with us.

I had spent most of the afternoon in my bedroom. I had gone up soon after lunch, and I had repaired my manicure and brushed my hair, and then I had got some paper and a pencil and sat down at a table near the window and made some sketches of wedding dresses. I had drawn a series of nondescript brides and labeled each of them *Mrs. Philip Holcomb*. Then I had tried to draw a picture of Philip, but I am a poor artist and it did not come out very well. The face looked like a cross between Dick Tracy and the mad professor in the horror movie, so I decided to quit trying to make it look like Philip at all. I put whiskers on the chin, and a mustache on the lip, and I made the hair stand straight up above the forehead. Finally, I looked at my watch and it was five o'clock, and it occurred to me that Emily and Tavean would be starting the cocktail hour and that I had better go downstairs and start it with them.

But from the living room there was no sound of voices. I remember that I went to my bedroom door and opened it a crack and heard nothing. I had no suspicions. I thought simply that the time had slipped up on them as it had on me, and I went to the bathroom and took a quick shower, dressed without delay, but without haste either, and went downstairs. The living room was empty. But still I did not suspect anything. People talk of feminine intuition, but looking at that clean and vacant parlor, I felt no twinge at the edge of my consciousness, my heart did not stand still, it skipped no beat. I went in and I almost sat down. It crossed my mind that I might make my own cocktail, but then I decided that it was not very ladylike to drink alone and that I had better find Tavean. In innocence, I crossed the hall and went through the library. And the library, comfortable and prim, had no message for me either; the tables were neatly dusted, the chairs were in their proper arrangement, Great-grandfather's old papers had been put away. But I went on and found the door to Tavean's room open, and beyond that door the bedroom was a mess. Drawers were pulled out. There were a few old shirts and socks flung on the bed. Most of the clothes were missing from Tavean's closet.

I stopped very still and listened once more, tried to catch some sound of life in the house, but the house was silent. So now I did suspect; I had been pretty slow, but now my mind was racing. I was catching on. I went back out into the hall, climbed the stairs, and walked down to Father's and Emily's room, knocked and got no answer. Then I rapped on the door panel again, a little louder this time, and waited and knocked again and called out, "Emily." Finally I opened the door and went in.

Here, I had to search about a little. For one thing, when a woman comes to the country, she brings more clothes than a man does. And if she stays there for a while, she has clothes sent up; so when she decides to make a precipitate departure, you cannot tell at once whether she has gone by just looking in her closet. Then, too, Emily was very neat and she had left no drawers hanging out, no discarded garments strewn around, no door open. But Emily herself was not here and her suitcases were gone. I looked for a couple of dresses that I had seen her wear and I could not find them. So now I knew, or thought I did at least, and I searched around trying to find a note, but they had not left us any message.

I do not know exactly what I felt at that moment. Later, I thought many things and accused both of them of many sins and blamed them in a thousand ways for the suffering they had caused us. Now, I could only think of Father who would be coming home from Van Buren soon, and I could not let him discover the truth for himself. I would have to tell him.

I would have to go downstairs and place myself by a window and watch in the darkness for the lights of his car and hope that they would not be his lights after all, but the lights of Tavean's Thunderbird returning. I would have to go down and not have that drink, not dare have anything more than a cigarette, because I couldn't bemuse my brain with alcohol, I couldn't let that vain hope become too big. I would have to remain convinced that they were really gone, that they were not coming back—at least not tonight—and I would have to be the one to break the news to Father.

So I did that. I took my seat in the living room and I watched. Soon the lights did appear. The car stopped and it was Father's car, and then that handsome, plagued, and hopeful man was in the living room. He appeared in the house with a smile on his face; he had accomplished his business, the tombstone would be moved to Adams' Rest. Maybe it was a small smile. I am sure that under the pressure of the last few days' events, he was not joyful. But compared with what he was going to be, he was the happiest man in the world and, knowing what he did not know, being aware of what he was ignorant about, I suppose I found him looking blissful. I suppose I had expected him to wear the mask of tragedy, but he did not. In a perfectly normal voice he said, "Hello, my dear. I did not mean to be so late. Where are the others?"

"Father," I said, "sit down. Let me give you a highball."

Now there was a look of apprehension on his face and I cannot tell you how my own face looked. Filled as I was with pity for Father, and with shock, and with anger, it must have shown something.

Father said, "What is it? What's the matter?"

For an instant I could not tell him. For a short space of silence I could not speak. I had prepared myself for this moment of agony. I had sat by the window waiting for him to come, knowing that I would have to say to him, *They are gone, Father. Tavean and Emily have gone away.*

Once or twice I had even said these words over, not aloud, but in a whisper; I had practiced my inflection, I had tried the tone of my voice. Now, my practiced voice delayed; then flatly it said, "Father, Tavean has gone."

Oh, I should have done it all at once. Doctors know about that. They use the lance or the probe swiftly; they subject you immediately to the worst of the pain. Timidly, I had told Father only part of what had happened, and in telling only part, I had given him hope.

"Tavean is gone, then," Father said softly. He frowned but his face did not really fall. "I had hoped that Tavean would not have to go . . . would not feel it necessary to go. But it will not make much difference. Perhaps we will all be able to leave here pretty soon."

"Father," I said, and felt like weeping. "It is more than that. Emily is gone too. They have gone together, I suppose, but I don't know where."

He did not answer. Just by looking at him, you could not tell that he understood, you could not be sure that he knew just what had happened. You read of physical transformations; of hair that turns gray overnight, of faces that assume the appearance of death, but Father simply stood and stared at me rather vacantly. I remember that I watched him very closely. Maybe I thought that he would go to pieces someway; dissolve in tears, or slump down on the couch, or tear his hair and groan and curse life's darkness. I noted how precisely his tie was knotted, how whitely his shirt collar shone in the light, how clean and free of lint were the lapels of his jacket. His face, too, was very clean and neat and it retained most of its color. His eyes were mystified, but they did not yet show pain.

"Tavean?" he said softly, questioningly, "Emily? Both of them gone?"

"Yes, sir," I said. "Let's sit down, Father."

He did not move.

"Today?" he said, his voice louder, more strained. "Left today? Together?"

"I think so," I said. "They must have."

"Then why didn't you stop them?" he shouted. "Don't you care enough about me to have done that? Couldn't you at least have made them wait until I got here?"

It was unfair for him to blame me, and momentarily I was angry—not so much at him as at Tavean and Emily.

"No," I said, "I couldn't. I was in my room and they didn't tell me they were going."

He was beginning to show more emotion now. He was hurt and he did not know what to do. He put his hand in his pocket and took out a package of cigarettes, but then he held the package and looked at it as if he did not know what cigarettes were or as if he could not read the lettering on the wrapper. I caught his arm and pushed him gently toward the sofa.

"Sit down," I said, "and I'm going to get you a drink. We'll both have a drink and I'll tell you all I know about it."

The little cocktail cart had been set out in the dining room. There was ice in the bucket and whiskey on the tray, but I did not take time to push the cart back into the living room. I grabbed a bottle and a couple of glasses and I poured a long straight one for Father and one not much shorter for myself. Then I took a big swallow and the whiskey burned and I almost lost my breath; I gulped a few times like a fish, without speaking.

Finally, I regained my voice and told him how I had been to Tavean's and Emily's room and found their bags and some of their clothes missing.

"Maybe they didn't go together," Father said. "Maybe they both just decided to leave. You didn't see them."

"They had to leave together, Father," I said. "Emily doesn't have a car up here. Only one car is missing."

"She wanted to go to Nashville," Father said. "She wanted to get away from here and Tavean consented to drive her. She must have left a note. You overlooked it."

"All right," I said. "Let's look again. But I don't think so."

And he did not act as if he really believed that Emily had left him a note, for when we got to the bedroom, his search was anything but thorough. He moved into the room which was fully dark now, paused, with only the light from the hall at his back, and waited until I crossed the floor and touched the lamp switch. He stood still for a moment longer, blinking once or twice and gazing vaguely about. Then he moved slowly and I followed him. He went into the dressing room, paused there and opened the closet door, looked inside but touched nothing, and shut the door carefully. He turned into the bathroom, his step measured, and looked blankly at the shower stall, the tub, the lavatories, the commode. Then he went back into the bedroom and stood by the bed and reached down and brushed his hand lightly back and forth along the counterpane.

"I don't see it," Father said. "Did you look in the drawers?"

"No," I replied.

He did not look in the drawers either. In that same slow and measured step, he left the room and descended the stairs. He returned to the living room and sat down and poured himself a drink and drank it. He emptied the glass and then sat holding it in his hand, turning it round and round, and running his finger over the etched initials. He sat and looked at the glass for a long time. Then he put the glass back on the table and wet his lips and blinked his eyes once more, and gazed absently about once more as he had done in the bedroom.

Finally he said, "Anne, I don't know what to do."

I could not help it. My eyes filled up with tears. The tears spilled over. I know that a woman's role is that of comforter. I know that a woman should be strong to endure, cheerful in the face of adversity, a source of power in the time of the heart's loss and anguish. But if Father did not know what to do, who could tell us what direction our lives ought to take, who could guide our footsteps? In tears, I asked myself this and, of course, I knew the answer, and foolishly perhaps—but foolishly or not—I told him.

"There is only one thing you can do," I said. "Whatever comes of this. However all this ends, you will have to forgive them."

"Forgive them!" he said angrily. "My son? My wife? forget what they have done to me? Pretend that it did not happen?"

"Oh, no," I said. "Not pretend anything. Just forgive them."

"Do you forgive them?" he asked.

I shook my head.

"But you intend to? Is that it? Before you even see them again? Before you hear what they have to say, you make up your mind to forgive them?"

"Yes," I said.

"Is that all you can say to me?" he asked. "After all these years of kneeling in church and burning candles? Is that all?"

"I don't know," I said. "Maybe it is. Maybe it is enough. I just don't know."

He was silent for a moment. "Anne, Anne," he said. "Don't let me argue with you. Don't let me fuss at you and make you angry. Oh, don't let me, for I cannot lose you, too."

Then the call came through from the Nashville hospital. I remember not the words, but the tone of the voice—a female voice that was neither sympathetic nor callous, only noncommittal. She could not tell me how badly they were hurt, she could not tell me how the accident had happened. She knew only that Tavean and Emily had been picked up by an ambulance fifteen miles north of Nashville on the Clarksville highway. They had got back to the city and gone fifteen miles beyond that, fifteen miles on the other side, away from us. Now, Emily was in the emergency room and Tavean had already been taken upstairs to surgery.

I did not think I could do it. Once more, I did not believe that I could tell him. I had been the bearer of evil tidings once that day, and then there had been time to prepare myself against his sorrow. Now, I replaced the phone in its cradle and hesitated, looking at the space that divided me from Father; the twenty feet of library, the ten feet of hall, and ten seconds to walk this distance and be in the living room with him, and tell him what I knew. I must wait, I thought. I must find a way to say it cautiously, gently. And I knew all the time that there was no way, that the power of words is grossly overestimated. Language can change no fact, can soften nothing. You speak and you make your meaning clear and the meaning is all.

So I moved. I put one foot in front of the other; the act of walking, conscious and careful like the clumsy locomotions of a child. I remember thinking, hoping that maybe something would save me. That maybe it was all a mistake, that perhaps before I got to the library door, the phone would ring again and the same cold, female voice would say that she had been wrong about Tavean, that he was not hurt, that Tavean was all right. But, of course, the phone did not ring. I reached the hall in dead silence, with even my footsteps making no sound on the carpet, no noise here of burning fire or ticking clock. And then I was back in the living room and I told him.

I said, "Father, they had an accident. They are at the hospital in Nashville. Both of them were hurt."

There was nothing for him to show now. There was no way for him to look any sadder than he already appeared. A while ago, I had stood in this same room and told him that Tavean and Emily had gone, and for a while he had shown nothing. I had sat here with him and had a drink, I had gone with him upstairs to look for a note, and I had seen the expression of pained vacancy come gradually into his eyes. I had seen the color of his flesh change, I had seen his hand tremble. He sat before me now, his face still ashen, his eyes blank and rimmed in red, a little patch of hair standing up on his head, the skin very white around his nostrils.

"No," he said, breathlessly, "not Tavean. Not Emily."

I leaned over him and put my hands on his shoulders. "Father, I am so sorry. But they are hurt. We had better go to Nashville."

I helped him get into his coat. When he had come in, he had come directly into the living room, and he had thrown his coat and hat across a chair. I picked up the coat and held it for him, held the sleeves down to his arms that he stuck stiffly out and pushed the coat up over his back and told him to button it. Then I handed him his hat and went upstairs to get a coat for myself and came back down and he was waiting for me with the front door open.

"I can't drive," he said. "Can you drive? I don't feel like driving."

I took the keys from him and we got in the car and started. It was raining again. Our lights reflected dully from the wet, black pavement. Raindrops splashed and rattled against the car.

"I'm sorry," Father said. "I don't think I could drive. I don't think it would be safe."

"It's all right," I said, "I don't mind driving."

After a while he said, "I'm not able to drive. It's a weakness in me, but I don't think I could."

We went on. We passed through Van Buren and got to the wide, concrete Nashville highway. I pressed down on the accelerator. The rain splattered a little harder against the windshield and the engine hummed.

"Don't go too fast," Father said fretfully. "That's the trouble with Tavean. He never knew the proper way to drive a car. He always drives too fast."

Then there was a mile or two more of silence, and Father said, "How badly do you think they are hurt?"

"I don't know," I replied. I had already told him all the woman on the telephone had told me. "They had to do some surgery on Tavean. I expect they'll be able to tell us more when we get there."

I prayed that Tavean would be all right. I drove along that rain-swept road and asked God to preserve Tavean, to spare him to us. I kept asking God to let him live. I kept repeating the same prayer over and over in my mind, but I did not pray for Emily. It occurred to me that I ought to pray for her, but I could not bring myself to do it. I just kept on asking God to make Tavean all right.

When we got to the hospital and went in, there were a few people waiting in the emergency room, but we could not find a nurse at once. There was a desk, but there was no one behind it, and none of the people waiting around on the benches knew where the nurse had gone. We stood there helplessly, not knowing what to do. A loud-speaker system kept calling different doctors, but the speaker did not tell the doctors where to go. It just called their names and the names were indistinguishable to me. An orderly came through the room, pushing a cart loaded with bottles, but he did not know where the nurse was, and he could not tell us anything about Tavean and Emily. He went out and, finally, after what seemed like a long time, the nurse came back. She was very young and small and, in a demure way, rather pretty. She was a blond with fair skin and thin features.

"I'm sorry," she said. "It's a busy night. It must be the rain."

Emily, she told us, had been taken up to a room. She had been asleep when she left the emergency room, under sedation. The nurse could not tell us how badly Emily was hurt. We would have to talk to the doctor. The doctor would tell us whether we could see her. Concerning Tavean, the nurse knew only that he had been taken to surgery. She made a couple of phone calls and told us to go to another part of the hospital, to another corridor, and talk to the nurse on duty there.

It was a long way through the hospital. We had to go out into a hall and ride an elevator up to the main floor and then walk for about a block to another elevator. Then we rode up to the seventh floor and got out and found another nurse and this one was old and gray and she appeared very competent. She looked as if she knew her job very well; she looked as if she had been working as a nurse for a long time, but like the first nurse, she would not tell us much about Tavean and Emily. They had been seen first by a house man, a resident who was on duty that night in the emergency room. The resident—who was still busy in the emergency room and could not be disturbed, could not talk to us—had done what he thought needed to be done for Emily. She was in a room on this floor, resting comfortably. The nurse thought that we could see her soon, but she would have to check with the resident when he had a spare moment.

Tavean apparently had needed more attention than the house man was capable of giving him. The resident had sent out a call for a neurosurgeon and there had been one, a Dr. Goldman, already in the hospital. He had taken Tavean up to surgery, where, so far as the nurse knew, Tavean was now.

"Why would he need a neurosurgeon?" Father asked.

"I don't know, sir," the nurse said. "You'll have to talk to the doctor."

"Listen," Father said, "you've been around hospitals a long time. You don't call a neurosurgeon to set a broken leg. What do you need one for?"

"I'm sorry," she said firmly. "I don't know. The doctor will have to tell you."

"Call Dr. Anderson," Father said. "Call Dr. Horace Anderson and ask him to come over here."

Father and I waited while the nurse made the phone call. She was able to reach Dr. Anderson and he said he would come. Then, we went back up the hall to a little waiting room which, being in the private pavilion, was cleaner than the lobby of the emergency room and better furnished. There were easy chairs, and draperies at the windows, new magazines on the glass-topped tables and crystal ashtrays, and prints on the walls. We could not sit down. That is, we could not stay sitting down; we would lower ourselves onto the soft cushions of the couch, but we could not remain there. One of us would get up and walk to the window, and the other would get up, too, and go look out the door.

Then the nurse came and told us that Emily was still asleep, but that we might go in and see her.

"What about Tavean?" Father said, "what about Mr. Adams?"

"I only talked to the doctor on the telephone," she said. "He's too busy to come up right now. He'll come when he can and tell you all about it."

She waited to take us to Emily's room, but neither of us moved.

"Father," I said and touched his arm.

Father looked down at the floor and shivered slightly. Through the cloth of his coat, I felt his body tremble. Very softly, he said, "I can't."

Then he said, "Horace Anderson might come. One of the other doctors might come. I've got to be here to find out about Tavean."

"I'll wait here," I said. "If I get any news, I'll come tell you."

His red eyes met mine in a look of infinite pain. "Don't you see?" he said. "I can't leave. I'm his father."

"You come, my dear," the nurse said.

I squeezed Father's hand and followed her along the corridor to a door and through the door into a room that was dimly lighted. With no flowers and no books, no cosmetics on the dressing table or box of candy by the bed, the room looked very bare. There was only a thermos pitcher of water, a glass turned down.

The nurse fussed for a moment around Emily. She was being given some liquid—saline, I guess—intravenously, and the nurse checked the needle that was taped to Emily's arm and smoothed the cover. Then the nurse left and I stood by the bed and looked at Emily.

She had been banged up. One side of her face was badly bruised and there were light scratches in the swollen, blue flesh. There was a bandage on her head just below the hairline, and the edge of another bandage showed on her arm beneath the rough, hospital gown. Emily looked different, hurt, and yet, in sleep, she looked a great deal the same. The silver hair glowed softly, the regular features retained their beauty, the flesh on her neck was very white and smooth.

I looked at her and knew that she would live, that she would come out of this hospital bed in a day or a week, and in a month or so be as exquisitely beautiful, as ineffably appealing to every man who crossed her path, as she had been the first time I had ever seen her. I gazed at her and I thought of Tavean lying somewhere upstairs, Tavean lying under the bright lamps, swathed in sheets, with no telling what part of his body laid open to the surgeon's vision, to endure the scalpel's fine excision, the needle's thrust. I thought about Tavean and thought that he might die, and I looked at Emily and knew that if he did die it would be her fault, and I knew that I hated her. I did not want to do anything to her. I did not want to be a child again and have her awake and whole so that I might act like a child again and pull her hair. I did not even want her revived that I might perform some act of adult cruelty; I did not want to say to her, *You did this to Tavean, you may have killed him,* and see then the fear and suffering flood her eyes. I did not want this and I did not want her dead. I just hated her purely, almost abstractly, beyond any thirst for revenge, beyond all contempt and recrimination. She lay breathing shallowly with the clear liquid dripping into her vein, and somewhere beneath her handsome breasts, her heart was beating. That was all right with me. Let it beat. Let it pump away or let it stop. I would go on hating her.

I left the room and went back to the lounge to wait with Father. Dr. Anderson had already been there. He had gone up to the operating room to find out what was being done to Tavean and how Tavean was standing the operation. Apparently, it would not be much longer before we knew something now, but now every minute would go that much more slowly. Father and I sat down, and I took out a cigarette and Father lighted it for me.

"How is Emily?" he asked, half absently, his tone only half interested. He was watching the doorway.

"Fine," I replied. "She's bruised up a little bit. I gather she may even have a concussion. But she's going to be fine." My voice was not angry or sympathetic. It was merely flat.

We were silent for a moment and I suppose he couldn't stand it any longer, couldn't endure the silence that went with the waiting, without even the sound of that speaker system calling doctors, that we had had in the emergency room. He had to say something, I suppose, to hold himself together, and he talked about Emily.

He said, "Did I ever tell you how I met Emily?"

"No, sir," I replied.

Then he said, "No, not how I met her, that is not how it began."

He put his hand to his mouth, held it there very tightly; with his thumb and his fingers, he squeezed the flesh of his cheeks. Then he removed his hand and shook his head and resumed, "It was one afternoon downtown. I got on the elevator and she was already on, already standing over in one corner. I thought at first only how young she looked and how very beautiful and, for some reason, I wanted to hear her talk. That's silly, isn't it? I mean, I know what the psychologists say, I know about Freud. But it's funny that whatever motive, desire, I had would manifest itself in just that way. I thought if once I could have a conversation with her, hear her speak, hear the tone of her voice, and what she talked about, then—but I don't know what then. I hadn't planned ahead. I just wanted to hear her." He paused. Then he said, "That's one of the first things I noticed about your mother, the way she talked, and with Emily it was the same way. It was almost like history . . ."

He broke off and stared at me, his eyes open wide in an expression of pained discovery. Then we both looked at the door, for the doctors were with us.

There was Dr. Anderson in ordinary business dress and beside him, a tall, fair, middle-aged man in a green scrub suit. He had removed his gloves, but he still wore the green trousers, the long green gown buttoned tightly at his wrists, the close-fitting green hat. His mask was white and it hung loose and limp around his collar. He was Dr. Goldman. He had regular features and he wore rimless spectacles. What hair I could see around his ears was turning gray. He and Dr. Anderson told us that everything possible had been done for Tavean. But he had not survived the operation. Tavean was dead.

A little later, we left the hospital. Dr. Anderson went with us to the house in Belle Meade, to the home that we had not used as a home for several weeks now. He gave Father a sedative, and he called Mr. Rathbone to go get Tavean's body, and then he sat with me for a while in the den and tried to comfort me. He wanted to help, but there was nothing he could do, now that Father had gone to bed and was sleeping. Dr. Anderson and I sat and talked, and when I insisted, he told me about Tavean, how Tavean had sustained a head injury and how the wonder was that he had lived long enough to get to the hospital. There had been too much brain damage for him possibly to have lived. Dr. Anderson wanted to give me a sleeping pill, but I did not want one. There would be things to do tomorrow, and tomorrow would come whether I slept tonight or didn't sleep. Whether I slept or whether I didn't, nothing would be changed.

Later, somewhat reluctantly, Dr. Anderson left. I stayed up for a while in the den, and then I went upstairs and undressed and sat down in my room and smoked a cigarette. Then I got in bed and lay quiet for a while, with the lights turned off. For a long time I lay quiet and wakeful. Finally, I dozed off and woke again, dozed and woke, and when I would wake up and find the room dark, I would wish it were morning. I kept wishing for the morning to come, so I could get up and do what I had to do, and once or twice I turned on the light and looked at my watch to make sure that it was not morning, and it was not. The last time I awakened, I must have been dreaming, for I sat up in bed with my cheeks wet with tears and I was still crying and I could not stop. I lay back down on the pillow and cried and cried, and when I woke up the next time it was day.

I got up and put my clothes on. I searched around in the closet until I found a plain black dress and a black hat with a simple black veil, and I walked along the hall and listened at Father's door. I went downstairs and told the butler to listen for Father and to stay with Father if he woke up, and then I got in the car and drove to the undertaker's and picked out the casket. I called the priest and made arrangements for Tavean's funeral, and then I called Van Buren and arranged for the digging of Tavean's grave.

When I got home, Father was awake and I went in to see him. He was still in his suite, but he had shaved and dressed, and he was sitting in front of his fire drinking coffee. I had some coffee, too, and I told him what I had done, and we sat and looked at each other sadly and he looked very old. He looked older than I had ever seen him, the lines in his face were deeper, his face was pale. With his lips pressed together, his hand nervous, restless, he looked very sorrowful. But I knew that he did not look as sorrowful as he was going to look, for the ordeal, the bereavement had just begun. There was still the day of waiting to live through and the funeral after that, and then the commencement of the real grief, and the long days and weeks and months of pain. And besides this, there was

Emily, who was still Father's wife, and I wondered if she knew yet that Tavean was dead.

Tavean's body was brought to the house a little before lunchtime. But by then the house had already begun to fill up with people, some of them coming to stay a few minutes, and others coming in to sit down and stay a long time. Flowers were beginning to arrive. When I went up and got Father and came down with him for him to look at Tavean, we moved through a kind of confusion that was hushed and quiet. We passed old friends who spoke to Father, men and women who had nothing to say except that they were sorry, and nothing to do except to kiss Father's cheek or to shake his hand. Then everybody stood back while Father looked at Tavean, and Father looked in the casket and cried and went back upstairs.

He stayed upstairs for the rest of the day, and I was alone with nobody to help me, really, for friends cannot do much to help you, no matter how hard they try, and the servants could not help. I wished that Philip were with me. I wished that he had never gone to look for Great-grandfather Adams' body, but he had gone. I had tried to reach him but he had left town and I did not know where to find him. Once, late in the afternoon, I caught myself wishing that Tavean would help me, and then I remembered suddenly that it was Tavean who was dead. I had not really forgotten this, of course, but it was a kind of forgetting, an almost forgetting, and I felt guilty. I went in and looked in the casket again, stood for a while looking in at the handsome boy who used to be my brother, who was still my brother, but who now was dead. I looked at the head resting on the quilted pillow; I looked at the still, white hands that were laid out neatly, one across the other. And I did not cry this time. I felt too bad.

That night I was called to the telephone and it was Philip. He was in a little town in Alabama.

"Darling," he said, "how are you?"

I did not answer. I could not tell him how I was. There were no words to describe how I was, for you do not pick up the telephone and say, *My heart is broken.* And for some reason, I could not tell him at once that Tavean was dead. I did not reply to his question. I simply said, "Philip." I called his name.

"Listen," he said, "I've been trying to get you. I called Adams' Rest. I thought you would be there."

"No," I replied. "We had to come home."

He caught now the sorrow in my voice. "Anne?" he said. "What's the matter, darling?"

I said, "It is Tavean. He was killed in an accident. He is dead."

There was a short silence.

"Tavean?" Philip asked. "Did you say Tavean?"

"Yes," I replied. "Oh, darling, please come home."

"I'm so sorry," he said. "I'll leave now. I'll be there in the morning."

"Do," I said. "Oh, do come. But be careful."

"I will," he said. "Poor baby."

He did not seem to be willing to hang up. I wanted him with me. I wanted him to start to Nashville this very instant, but he did not seem to want to leave the phone.

"All right," I said. "I'll be waiting for you, darling."

"Anne," he said, "there is one other thing. I found General Adams. But he wasn't killed at Van Buren. It wasn't like Horatio thought. I don't know what to do. I don't know whether to tell him what I found out or not."

"Don't worry about that," I said. "Whatever it is cannot be as bad as what has happened. Don't worry about that right now. Just come on home."

I hung up the phone and sat for a moment beside it, looking at the phone, feeling very tired. Then I got up and went back out to the living room. I went back to the front of the house where people were congregated, where the flowers were banked on each side of the casket, where Tavean lay.

9

The Quest of Philip Holcomb

Well, I had to do it. There was a time—according to the stories—when all you had to do to win the lady was go out and kill the dragon and then you would be welcomed back to the castle with open arms. There was even a time when it could be done for money; you could raise the cash to save the home place and stand by with the girl in your arms and smirk, while the villain talked about being foiled and tore up the mortgage. But there was nothing easy like that for me. If I wanted to live in peace and harmony with Anne, not to mention Horatio who would be my father-in-law, I had to find the body of a dead general.

So, knowing that I would have to do it, I did not delay. On the afternoon of the day that we opened the grave, I drove back to Nashville and went directly to the state archives and started my search. I took what you might call the academic approach to the problem; I got the muster roll of General Adams' brigade and I checked every name on the muster roll against the card catalogue in the library.

Every time I came across a book or letter or manuscript written by one of General Adams' soldiers, I stopped and read what that soldier had had to say about the Civil War. I skimmed through some good books and a lot of bad ones. I read some interesting letters and some very silly letters; I wasted my time over manuscripts that were almost illegible. And all this took me four days. Four long days I spent, missing Anne and straining my eyes, and cursing Horatio, and when I was done I had nothing. I had followed the academic approach to a blank dead end.

That night, I went home to my apartment and thought about my alternatives and I almost decided to give up the search. I considered how little it meant to me, personally, to find General Adams. I didn't care where he was buried and, except that she loved her father and wanted to see him happy, I don't think Anne cared much either. What I had done, I had done for Horatio, and it occurred to me that I had done enough. I could go back to Adams' Rest and say, *I can't find him. I have tried. I have done what I could. But I have failed.*

Except I knew that I couldn't do that, not because of Horatio, but because of myself. I was a professional or claimed to be. I called myself an historian, and I had some college degrees and a small bibliography to prove it; I gave lectures at a university and I was supposed to be good. I was obligated not only to know something about history, but to be able to find out new things about the past; and here I was, after four days of effort, feeling sorry for myself and giving up.

I would have to keep working and I knew that the smartest way would be to start down another of the academic roads; logically, the next step would be to check name by name in orderly sequence, the same muster roll against another file in the library—a catalogue of items which the archives did not have but which were known to be in existence. But doing it this way would take a whole lot longer than another four days. The manuscripts listed in this catalogue were scattered from one end of the country to the other, and a lot of them were in private collections. I'd have to write for photostats or telephone the people who owned the papers, and maybe have parts of documents read to me over the phone. Doing it that way would take too long. I would have to search my mind and discover a short cut.

I almost went to work on the basis of geography. It occurred to me that I might start out with the men who had come from Van Buren, but there was a flaw in that approach. One might think that men who come from the same place and go to an army would be good friends after they got to the army. But I remembered that I went to the Marines with some boys from Nashville who were good fellows, I suppose, but not very congenial. I was closest to boys from places like Texas and Virginia and Maine and Minnesota. I thought a little more about myself and I remembered that, when I was a private I consorted with other privates, and when I was a lieutenant I sought the company of other lieutenants, and I decided that if I had ever got to be a general—which the Marine Corps can thank God never happened—I would have sat at the general's table when I went to the club. So far, so good. But given combat conditions, and Civil War conditions at that —no officers' mess and the army all spread out in the field and no motor pool—there wouldn't be enough generals in the same immediate neck of the woods to get together every night and tell old stories.

I quit thinking so much about myself and started thinking hard about the Confederate Army. I remembered how Forrest had had his personal guard, and how Jeb Stuart had had a couple of musicians always handy and von Borcke for comic relief, and how Jackson had kept tabs on Lacy and Pendleton and Dabney just to be sure, I suppose, that when he knelt down at night, he wouldn't be the only man in that acre of God's world who was praying. The place to look was General Adams' staff and the next morning I got the staff names and ran them through the catalogue.

Out of a list of fourteen staff officers and six men who had been more or less permanently attached to headquarters as couriers, I came up with two items; a diary in the possession of a lady in Eau Claire, Wisconsin, and some letters written by a Major Pearson which were owned by Thurman Shoffner of Hawthorne, Alabama. I tried Mr. Shoffner first because he was closer. Any phone call I made would be a gamble and I didn't want to lose too much at the very start.

I gave the operator my message and dropped in the quarters; soon the phone rang at the other end and I had Mr. Shoffner. He sounded like an old man. Of course, you can't always tell over the telephone and his voice was strong and deep enough and he didn't sound senile. But there was something old-fashioned in the way he talked. I asked him if he were Mr. Shoffner and he said, "I am, sir," and then I told him who I was and where I was calling from. He said he knew some people in Nashville, but he didn't know any Holcombs. I listened while he named over his Nashville acquaintance, and I had to say I had heard of some of them, but I wasn't connected with any of them. That was his word, connected; I hadn't heard anybody use it that way in a long time.

After all the name and family talk, I told him what I wanted, and the line went dead. From Mr. Shoffner's end, there was no sound, not even the faint whisper of the old man's breathing. I waited; it occurred to me that he had a right to a little silence. It's not every day or year or lifetime, probably, that somebody calls you up long distance and says, *I'm sorry to bother you, but I've lost a body. It's been lost for about a hundred years now, but I just got around to looking for it. I wonder if you could tell me where it is.* These are not the words I used, of course, but this was my meaning. I could understand his not replying right away.

"Let me get this straight," he said at last. "You opened the grave in the Confederate cemetery and found no remains."

"Yes, sir," I said, "and we'd like to locate the body. We thought maybe there'd be something in the Pearson correspondence that would give us a clue."

"I don't know," he said doubtfully.

"Could I see the letters?"

There was another long silence.

"Maybe that won't be necessary," Mr. Shoffner replied finally. "Hold the phone a minute."

When he came back on the wire, he read me part of a letter written by Major Pearson, who, incidentally, had been his mother's father. Major Pearson had been a good friend of General Adams. He had mentioned General Adams often in his letters home. But this, according to Mr. Shoffner, was the next to last reference to General Adams in the Pearson correspondence. The letter had been composed on the afternoon of November 26, 1864. The army had stopped to camp after a day of marching. Major Pearson said that he and General Adams were going to pass the night in the Dedman residence, just south of Columbia, Tennessee. The last mention of General Adams was that he had been killed in the Battle of Van Buren.

I thanked Mr. Shoffner and hung up the telephone.

Well, this was something anyway. I had never gone in much for old Tennessee houses unless they had figured prominently in the war. But being a Ph.D. in history has its advantages. I knew where to look. I got back into the archives just before they closed for the night, and I got a couple of books on historical Tennessee homes, and I found it. There was its picture; a white brick, columned mansion, not so imposing as Adams' Rest maybe, but plenty good enough to call home and not be ashamed to have your out-of-town friends drop in unexpectedly. It had a name—Elmview. And according to my source, some of the Dedmans still lived there.

I left the library and had dinner. Bright and early the next morning I got under way.

I gassed up my Plymouth and drove south, back through Van Buren, back past the painted soldier, past Adams' Rest, and I had a notion to stop and see Anne just for a little while. But I restrained myself. Business—even my kind of business—had to come before pleasure. I just looked at the house in longing and kept my foot on the accelerator.

Now lower middle Tennessee is beautiful country, horsy country; with the big white houses set back on their big, green lawns, and a few hundred yards down the gleaming white fence, the stables looking like the penthouse at the Ritz. It is not all like this, of course. There are poor people here like there are everywhere else, but for the man who lives in the big house or parties there on the weekend, it is fun three hundred and sixty-five days a year and a mighty pretty tax loss come next April. This is Tennessee's bluegrass country, and Columbia calls itself the "Dimple of the Universe."

Which is a fetching name, but not exactly accurate. I got to town about ten o'clock and, because the day was pretty and warm for December, I knew exactly what to do. I went to the courthouse to see the village loafers. I stopped my car and got out and I acted like I had all the time in the world; I said good morning and let them look me over. Then I asked where the old Dedman place was, and one of the men on the front bench got his mind off the integration fracas long enough to tell me.

It was off the main highway, but it was easy to find. I hit a macadam road and followed it for about a mile, and then I came up over a hill and there on the next rise was Elmview. It looked just like the picture in the book, two stories in the main section with full-length columns and a one-story wing on each side. There was a black top drive leading up to the front veranda and, off in the distance, in a field beyond the house, a herd of black Angus were grazing the winter fescue. I stopped my car and crossed the wide porch and rang the bell.

The door was opened by a girl about twenty or twenty-one years old. She had a round face and brown hair cut short, and the hair settled over her head like a loose cap. Her mouth was a little tight, her lips were a little thin, and this made her look intense or, perhaps, just curious. But I expect most of the boys she knew didn't often look at her face. She had on a red and white striped blouse cut low in the neck, and a pair of tight, red toreador pants, and red loafers. I told her my name and where I was from and she asked me to step inside. As it turned out, she thought I wanted to see the house. People came every now and then to look it over.

Before I could disabuse her, an old man moved into the entrance hall where the girl and I were standing. He was the girl's grandfather, I came to find out, and he had the same sharp look, though his jowls were sagging and his hair had turned gray. He was big, fat really, not so much in the stomach as all over. His arms and legs were big and round. On one of his feet, he wore a felt carpet slipper, and he walked with a cane.

His name was Albert Dedman, and he took me into a sitting room and I told him what I wanted. I sat down in the parlor with the old man and, if the gold brocade of the love seat had not been obviously new, the red of the drapes fresh and unfaded, you would have thought that it had not changed for a hundred years. The carpet on the floor matched the drapes, and there were some blue and white and gold Meissen vases on the mantelpiece, and all the wood in the room—the tables and the chair frames—was walnut. Without too much effort, you could see the old general sitting here, talking to the lady of the house; the general's uniform worn and the frogs on his sleeves tarnished, but the stars and the wreath on his collar would make up for that. In your imagination, you could see him, if you wanted to try—the wide forehead, the tired, blue eyes—even if you were a confirmed and somewhat cynical realist like me.

But I hadn't come to Mr. Dedman's Elmview to daydream. I told the old man who was really sitting here with me, his hands folded across his stomach, his slippered foot on a stool for comfort, that the last word we had of the living general was news that he had come here to have his supper, maybe, or to spend the night. I told him how we had lost the body, and I asked if he knew whether General Adams might have died here or been buried here or somewhere nearby.

All this disturbed Mr. Dedman, but I was prepared for that. Just hearing it over the telephone had startled Mr. Thurman Shoffner of Hawthorne, Alabama. Mr. Dedman puffed up. He blew out his cheeks and then let the air come popping out through his lips, so he sounded like a cross between a tired horse and an old-time steam engine. He wound up by coughing asthmatically and his face got red.

"I don't know anything about it," he said finally. "All that happened a long time ago."

"But you must know that he stopped here," I said. "He was a general. Your people would have remembered that. You must have heard the story."

"Lots of Confederate generals stopped here," he said, his

face still red, his voice angry. "We were loyal to the Confederacy. Many officers were taken in here, but I don't remember any General Adams."

He was lying now. Maybe not about General Adams, but about the salon his forebears had run for Confederate officers. Because during most of the war, this part of Tennessee was Yankee territory. But, of course, I couldn't point this out. I just sat for a while and looked at him and he looked at me.

"Do you have any records?" I said at last. "Any old diaries?"

"I don't have anything," he said. "I've already told you all I know. I can't help you."

So there was nothing for me to do but get up and move for the door. Because of his lame foot, maybe, or because he figured I knew my way, he did not come with me. He stayed in the parlor, puffing out his cheeks, and I walked into the entrance hall and made a discovery. Mr. Dedman and I hadn't been having a tête-à-tête after all. The girl had been just outside the parlor, listening to what we said. Now she smiled secretively and motioned for me to follow her.

She led me down the marble parquet, past the stairs, and we went into a den at the back of the house. This room had been remodeled, or maybe added. It was all glass on two sides, and you could see the elm trees, and the view, too; and outside, the day was beginning to darken. It was cloudy and there was a promise of rain.

But we were inside and all was bright. When I had rung the doorbell, the girl had apparently been back here reading. There was an easy chair with a table beside it, an ash tray and a coffee cup, both dirty, and spread open, face down, a copy of the *Partisan Review*. On the floor at the other side of the chair were a couple of issues of *The Nation*.

"How's vacation?" I asked.

"All right," she said. "I just got through classes yes . . . " Then she broke off and her eyes narrowed. They were gray eyes, bright and large, and she had long lashes. "Quit playing detective," she said. "It's not a crime to read, yet. Not even in Tennessee."

"I'm sorry," I said. "It was just sour grapes. There are some things I want to know that books won't tell me."

"That's why I called you back here," she said. "Your man, your General Adams was here. Grandfather and the rest of them won't talk about it. It's that Old South and magnolia business. He was here right enough. He died here. My great-grandfather killed him."

"What?" I said.

"Sure," she replied, leaning forward, staring at me intently. "He's still here, what's left of him. I suppose they wouldn't have told me except I found the grave."

It was going a bit too fast for me now. I raised my hand as high as my shoulder and waved it at her gently, palm out. "Wait a minute," I said, "wait a minute, Miss . . . "

"Charity," she said. "I'm Charity Dedman."

"Wait a minute, Charity," I said. "Go back a little."

"I found the grave," she said impatiently. Then she leaned back with a weary sigh and curled up in her chair.

"I just came upon it. It had been there in the woods

all the time, not more than a dozen feet off the bridle path, and I'd never noticed it. Then one day I rode by there, going slowly I suppose, and I looked and saw the mound and what was left of a wooden marker. I came home and asked whose it was, and when I threatened to go down there and dig and see if there really was anything buried, they had to tell me."

She paused and lit a cigarette. "You can bet they Goddamn well didn't want to tell me. They keep feeding me this stuff about respecting the Old South."

"All right," I said. "They told you. What?"

"About what happened," she said. "This general and some other fellow came here to spend the night. My great-grandfather was a boy then, too young to be in the army. He and his mother were the only ones here. During the night, this general tried to rape my great-grandfather's mother and my great-grandfather killed him."

"Tried to do what?" I said.

"Rape her," Charity said calmly. "It happens."

"Yes," I said, "it happens. But why?"

"Why?" she echoed. "Good God! Where have you been all your life? You sound like Grandfather."

Sitting there with that pretty, intense, bright girl, I remembered that I had been this young once. Once, I had believed that the world and the people in it were simple and that each human act had its single, identifiable human motive. Once, I too had been happily certain that I understood life.

"Show me the grave," I said finally.

"All right," she said. "Grandfather's going to be mad as

hell. But by now he knows I've told you. He's been sitting out there watching for your car to drive away."

Charity and I went out the back door, crossed a patio, went through the garden, and then walked over the fields toward the woods. We passed among the cows that were still grazing, and it was easy going, even for a city man like me. At this time of year, the grass was short. The ground was as smooth as the lawn out front, and I had Charity and my thoughts to keep me company. We walked in silence, and I thought of Horatio and wondered how he was going to like this story and whether he would want the body now. I thought of Anne and how she would have to help me break the news to her father. Charity and I walked, and from the trees in front of us, there was the sound of crows. A minute later, we flushed the crows and they rose, flapping slowly, black against the dull December sky.

Then we were on the bridle path, which was not as smooth as the fields had been, and a little later we were at the grave. It was, as she had said, half-hidden in the brush, grown over with buckbushes, but the growth on the grave was considerably younger than the bushes and trees that grew around it. What we were looking at was a grave all right. There are some things in life you know by their shape and a grave is one of them. The remnants of the marker that Charity had seen were gone.

"There it is," she said. "You can see how riding by, you wouldn't be likely to notice it."

"Yes," I said. I could see.

I stood by the grave of General Adams, and it occurred

to me that I ought to feel something, some joy or elation that the search had ended, or some embarrassment or chagrin over the way he had been killed. And I guess I did feel something, but for a while I didn't know what it was.

"Charity," I said, "when did they bury him here?"

"Right after my great-grandfather killed him," she replied. "That night. They finished before daylight."

"Yes, at night," I said. "And they buried him here because they didn't want anybody to know what had happened. Is that right?"

"Look," she said, "you're from this part of the country, aren't you? You know how they act about honor. And sex." She added this, not as an afterthought, but as a grand climax.

"Yes," I said, "and ever since that night they've been hating him."

"Yeah," she replied. "With a passion. Ever since, they've been hating his damned Confederate guts."

"All right," I said, "and I thank you. Now, let's go back before we get caught in the rain."

I didn't re-enter the house. I thanked Charity at the rear door and walked around through the side yard to the driveway and got in my car. I drove back to Columbia and put in a call for Mr. Shoffner. When he came to the phone, he sounded a little jollier or a little more apprehensive than he had the night before. His old voice had a little more life in it.

"You found him?" Mr. Shoffner said.

"Yes, sir," I replied. "At least, I found a grave and a girl who says he's in it."

"What was that?" he asked.

"A girl named Charity Dedman," I said. "She told me a story. It's not a very happy story. I'd like for you to hear it."

"Go ahead."

"Not on the telephone," I said. "I'd like to come down there."

He breathed deeply. Sitting there in the drugstore phone booth, I heard him sigh.

"All right," he said finally. "If you feel that way about it, come ahead."

I went to Hawthorne. It was raining when I left Columbia and that made the drive into Alabama take a little longer, but I had the time. Considering all that had happened, I needed the time to think over what Charity Dedman had told me and to get set in my mind the piece I meant to speak to Mr. Shoffner. What worried me was not that Charity had taken me into her confidence. She was at a rebellious age. For the last couple of years, she probably hadn't agreed with her family once, not even on the time of day or the price of tomatoes. She was fed up with the old julep-scented South; she had got the liberal view, like you get a fever, and she was shaking with an ague to tell all the scandal about the past. This was all right with me. This had been my good luck this morning.

What was wrong with the grave? If General Adams had been buried the night of his death, he had not been buried in a casket. He had been wrapped in a blanket maybe or covered in nothing at all, and he had been lowered in a hole and the dirt had been thrown in on top of him. But even if he had been buried in a casket, the casket would have rotted and the grave would have sunk. In a year or two, the grave would have leveled out again and in ninety years, it would have grown over, so you could not tell the new growth from the old. What bothered me was that you could find the grave, that you could see it there, shaped like, looking like a grave. Somebody had filled the grave after it had settled and, for a long time after General Adams' death, somebody had kept the grave site cleared. This was not to mention the marker which Charity told me about, but which I never saw. This was the problem I wanted to put to Mr. Shoffner.

When I got to Hawthorne, I stopped at a filling station and found out where Mr. Shoffner lived. The house was an old Victorian affair with curlicues and steeples and a railing around the porch and narrow glass windows on each side of the door. The maid led me into a parlor and it was what you would expect. In its way, it was as authentic as the living room at Elmview. There was a narrow, grate fireplace, a platform rocker, a large rosewood couch that was tufted and carved. On an easel near the the windows was a picture of a lady in outmoded dress.

Mr. Shoffner came in and shook my hand and gave me some sherry. He was a small man, short and slim, with a very pale and wizened face and a few strands of white hair that were almost invisible against his scalp's paleness. He had brown eyes and he wore pince-nez and there was a Masonic ring on his finger. He looked to be about eighty years old. He told me that he had been a lawyer but had now retired.

He sat down and crossed his short, frail legs, fingered his watch chain, and drank his wine; and I told him my story. I started with Horatio and our visit to the cemetery and I went on from there and tried not to miss a thing. Then I told him about the grave and how, for a long time, somebody had attended to it.

He got the point. "Yes," he said. His mouth was very small and he had a way of licking his lips before he spoke. The tongue flicked out as pink and delicate as a baby's. "Yes. And you wonder why they would take care of the grave of a rapist."

"Yes, sir," I said.

He was silent for a moment. Then he said, "Well, the chances are that he did not rape her. Major Pearson was my mother's father and I knew him, you see. He did not die until 1902. I know that he never thought General Adams had forced his attentions on the lady."

"Did he tell you about it?" I asked.

"Yes," he said, "after I was grown. You know how it is with an old man." Mr. Shoffner licked his lips and smiled. "You don't know. But when you are old, you think about the past. You think about the time when you were young and sometimes, things that happened years ago will begin to bother you. I expect this happened to Major Pearson. One day, when he was about as old as I am now—he was a little man, like I am, and I suppose I look a good deal like him—he told me about the death of General Adams. We were at his house in the country. I remember that it was August and the sky was very blue and we were sitting on chairs that had been placed in the shade of an oak tree.

"He told me that they had spent the night at the Dedman place and that most assuredly General Adams had been in the bedroom of the woman. He was shot there and he died with no clothes on. And, of course, in the presence of her son, the woman claimed that the general had tried to rape her. Major Pearson did not believe this. He was himself a light sleeper, even on the march, and he did not hear the woman call out. His room was across the hall from the woman's room and he heard no struggle. He heard only the shot and a space of silence that followed. He said that it seemed to him that the shot echoed forever through the house, and he remembered sitting up in bed, waiting for the reverberations to cease. It was, he said, as if he were under a spell, and could not move again until the noise of the gun had exhausted itself. He must not have hesitated for over a second or two, for when he got to the room, the general lay on the floor, his body still twitching. The boy still held the gun, an old rifle, empty now and pointing uselessly toward a corner, and the woman stood by the fireplace covered only in a sheet she had snatched from the bed.

"She claimed, of course, that the general had raped her, but what else would you expect her to say under the circumstances? She had her good name to protect. She had the boy's action to defend. What woman, no matter how depraved, likes to admit her impurity?

"But Major Pearson did not believe General Adams had raped her. That is why he rode on to Van Buren and did what he did. He sent word to his own brigade that they were to march without their general. Then he rode around his own troops and got to the head of the army. When the battle was joined, he made himself conspicuous, and reported to everyone he saw that General Adams was on the field. After the battle, he found a spot and broke the ground and marked the spot as the burial place of General Adams."

That was the story that Mr. Shoffner told me and it was a better story than the one I had got from Charity. It explained the present appearance of the grave. The woman had kept it.

"Yes," Mr. Shoffner said, "she would have felt some guilt. She would have done what she could at the grave to expiate it."

We were silent for a while.

Then Mr. Shoffner said, "But even so, what you have found will be a disappointment to Mr. Adams."

"Yes, sir," I said. "He's not going to like it."

"Let me tell you something," Mr. Shoffner said. "It comes to all of us. We are all weak sooner or later, but most of us live through it. Most of us survive to mend our ways. Do you know what I think happened to General Adams? I think the beauty of what he saw was too much to bear. He had lost his wife, and he knew that the South was losing the war, and he knew in his mind that his youth and the kind of life he had lived in his youth were over. He knew that in his mind, I say, but the heart is stubborn. The heart needs the image, the picture drawn, and in the beauty of Elmview and what we can suppose was the beauty of the woman, the heart understood. You are too young to comprehend the urgency. We all begin life believing that the world is ordered and centered around us. We interpret the worst catastrophes as lessons to our pride or tests of our endurance. We live through the flood or the storm or the fire and think—without admitting it aloud—that other men died that we might learn our lessons. We believe that we control our own fates, which is to believe that we can bend the world to our wills, and who can face being disabused on this head with equanimity?

"I know that General Adams used to sit around the fire at night, a tall man with beard turning gray, blue eyes, a wide forehead. He had a deep voice and it was his habit to recline on the ground, rest himself on his elbow and smoke when he had the cigars and chew on a twig or a blade of grass when he didn't. He would talk of the war and of the nation, but when he spoke, he was really speaking of himself.

"Major Pearson told me that on the night before the Battle of Atlanta, someone on the staff had got a jug of whiskey. They stayed up late talking and drinking, four or five men in a headquarters tent sitting around a table. They spoke of many things as men will and, after a while, there came a pause in the talk and General Adams, who had been a little morose all night, looked at each of them acutely. He turned his gaze from face to face, his eyes open in an expression of surprise, as if he had awakened suddenly from a deep sleep and found himself among strangers. Then in a strained voice, he said to a lieutenant who was sitting on his left, 'How old are you?' and the boy, who was twenty-three, told him. 'Are you married?' the general asked. And the boy said he was not married and the general was silent for a while. He took a drink and wiped his mouth and looked down at the table; then he raised his face again into the light. 'And what if you get killed?' he finally said to the boy. 'Young as you are, would you mind dying? Would it make any difference?'

"I am told that the boy blushed. Major Pearson said that he was a fair young man and that the color came red into his cheeks and his eyes glittered. 'Yes, sir,' he said. 'I do not want to die. I would like to live forever.' And the general said very softly, 'No. That's not what I meant. It's not your dying that really counts. It's all the rest that you have to go through. All the other dying and growing old and living.'

"And that is all he said. The other men left his tent. And he went to sleep or did not go to sleep. He had another drink or did not have it. Maybe if we knew what he did that night, we would have our answer. But, believe me, it is a hard thing to submit to the world. But he was not the only man who ever had to find that out or, as we know from the cleared grave, the only woman."

I waited a minute. Then I said, "I'd like to see a picture of the woman."

"Yes," he replied. "There is that, too. That might be all we needed to explain everything. That might make all this talk sound mighty foolish."

Well, that was it. I had my story and I thanked Mr. Shoffner. I shook his hand and got my coat and I drove to the town's only liquor store and bought a pint of bourbon. I took the bottle back to my car and I sat there and drank and listened to the rain fall and smoked and watched the windows fog. I tried to get a picture in my mind of the old general. I knew what he looked like from the portrait I had seen, but I wanted to get a vision of the fleshly man; I wanted to see him move, to hear his voice. I wasn't very successful. Sometimes you can read about General Lee and, after you go to bed, you will see General Lee in the dark, or you will dream and it is the Wilderness again and you are one of the soldiers. You can hear a story about someone you never saw and, for a moment, you will know how that person felt and you can feel the surge of blood and the quick heartbeat. But with General Adams, I never had much success. My thoughts kept wandering and I would see Horatio standing beside that empty grave, his face growing paler, his features more drawn, his mouth drawing tightly shut in an expression of infinite gloom and pain and disappointment. Maybe it was the whiskey, or maybe I just don't know how to concentrate, but that's the way it was.

After a while, I started the engine and drove to the nearest drugstore and telephoned Anne.

10

The Life and Times of Horatio Adams

I GRIEVED for Tavean, and grieved for him very deeply, and I continue to this day to sorrow for his death. But in the life of man, nothing is ever pure, not joy or love or even anguish, because life itself is never pure, never simple. Tavean was dead and, for a while, at least, I would have been almost content to have only the sorrow of his death to live with. But there was Emily, too, and there was the truth about my grandfather which Philip and Anne told me, and there was no way of putting either of these things out of my mind, because each of them had contributed, in a way, to the death of Tavean. During the day that followed the accident and the day after that when we buried Tavean, my mind pursued a tight and questioning circle, my recollection took me from one event of the past to another. Sometimes, I would go back in memory to my first meeting with Nancy, and I would think that if I had not been on that house party in Lexington, Kentucky, I would never have met Nancy, and now I would not be grieving over Tavean who was dead. But it was silly to go back this far, and silly, too, to dwell on the question of whether it is really better to have loved and lost; because what I wanted was not the sort of empty peace that I might have had if I had lived a bachelor, but the peace that I had almost had, that I thought I did have when Tavean was my son alive and I had loved him and felt myself secure in his affections.

Sitting in my own room upstairs, while Tavean's body lay in state in the drawing room, I would think of how I had first seen Emily—as I had thought of this and spoken of it to Anne the night before in the hospital—and I was sorry that I had ever seen her and sorrier still that I had married her. I wished that she were dead instead of Tavean. But, then, I would start thinking about my grandfather and I suppose I hated him most of all, because if he had behaved himself and died where he should have died and been buried where he should have been buried, then I might now have Tavean and Emily both. And even in my grief I knew that if Tavean were still alive, I would still love Emily.

These are the thoughts that filled my mind. And I guess, in a way, what I was doing was what I had done when I was a little boy and had gone to the turret room in the house on Russell Street. I was trying to convince myself that I was not Horatio Adams, just as years ago, I had tried to make myself believe that my mother and father had not died at sea, but, of course, I was unsuccessful. I couldn't deceive myself this time, either. I was indeed I. I sat through the funeral ceremonies, I rode in the procession to Adams' Rest, I saw the casket lowered into the grave, and the grave covered. And when I got back from the funeral, I went to the hospital to see Emily.

I did not want to see her. I did not think that I ever wanted to see her again. But I had to see her simply to tell her this, that, for my part, it was all over. She could go her way and do what she wanted to do and I would support her—I took pride in this; she would live on money from the man whose son she had killed—but I did not ever want to be with her again, live with her again, and it didn't matter to me whether she got a divorce or not, because I was through now. After what life had done to me, I was finished with letting myself love and letting my heart be broken.

I remember how I drove to the hospital with my palms sweating, my mouth set. I moved slowly through the traffic, made a slow entry to the parking lot, and walked like a very old man—which was the way I felt—across the street and down the sidewalk; slowly and alone, I moved through the winter day.

But I had not counted on what being in the hospital would do to me. It was not tears. It was not even weakness. Inside the building I stood firmly, my eyes dry. But, for a moment, I was immobilized and completely insentient. My muscles would not respond, my feet would not take me on along the corridor. I felt neither the inside warmth nor the draft of the door opening and closing behind me. Footsteps and voices for me made no sound and what I saw—the people, the information desk—registered clearly on my frozen brain, but the images had no meaning.

Then this passed and I moved in an agony of recollection which was not the blunt and numbing sorrow of all my torn and wasted years but the sharp and separate memory of that moment in the waiting room when the doctor had come and told us that Tavean was dead.

I did not think I could go through with it, but I did not stop. I found Emily's room and knocked on the door. I heard her voice bid me come in and I entered.

And it is strange how appearances change without really changing, how the eye colors whatever it sees, so the beloved object of yesterday becomes the trash which offends today's altered vision. For truly, Emily, the physical Emily, was the same. Oh, there was a small white bandage on her forehead and some slight discoloration on one of her cheeks. But these were little things and they did not matter. Dressed in a negligee, seated near a window, she was the same; the same magnificent body rested beneath the folds of silk, and the mouth, the nose, the eyes, the hair were no different. Now, when I saw her, nothing happened. There was no happiness and no great anger and no sorrow beyond that which I had brought with me, carried like a burden down the hallway into this room. And what were we to say, meeting again like this, after three days which, for me at least, had been longer than a season?

I sat down and I said, "Why did you do it, Emily?" That was, you see, the best that I could do. As if the reason, the explanation might mitigate the fact, call back the past, return Tavean to the company of the living.

She did not answer. She looked down and shook her head.

"Why did you do it?" I repeated.

She raised her eyes and said, "I don't know. Why did you?"

"I?" I said in astonishment. And then I knew that this was her female subterfuge. This is the way women behave; they change the subject, they accuse the accuser, they defend themselves by launching an attack.

I regarded her in silence for a moment. Her legs were crossed and she was swinging her foot, the white, heelless slipper dangling. Once this movement would have warmed my blood and made it race; now, her simple physical existence, the very displacement of her body in the chair, was for me an ultimate annoyance.

"I did nothing," I said. "I loved you and Tavean. It was you who left me to go with him. It was you who killed him."

"Oh, no!" she said, her face growing very pale, the bruise showing dark against the cheek's whiteness. "I didn't make him drive the way he did. I didn't make him have the accident. I didn't kill him. I wouldn't have killed him, not for anything in the world. I loved him."

"Loved him?" I echoed lamely. For I had not expected her to use these words. I had not believed that she would put the case so bluntly.

"Loved him?" I repeated harshly. "And I suppose he loved you. And I guess for you that was all that mattered, wasn't it?"

"Yes!" she said, leaning forward, her eyes bright and narrowed. "Yes! It was all that mattered! It is all that matters even now, even after . . . " And she broke off in tears.

She cried for a while and then, more quietly, she said,

"I don't know whether he loved me. He was just good and kind and he wanted me to be happy."

"Yes," I said bitterly, "just good and kind. And just young and handsome. No gray in his hair, no wrinkles in his face."

"No!" she said. "That made no difference."

"It must have," I replied, "because maybe I'm not good and kind, but God help me, I wanted you to be happy."

"You didn't," she said. "If you had, Tavean would be alive now. I would never have left you. Oh, oh," she moaned and she covered her face with her hands. "Oh, I'm sorry. I'm sorry he is dead. I would do anything to bring him back to life. I would have died myself to have him go on living."

'Stop!" I said, "hush!" but my voice was weak. My words were barely audible beneath the sound of her weeping. I felt the rising passion of my grief, which is the true passion, the true sense of the word that is commonly used to describe love and love's yearning and love's warm fulfillment. I felt the pain of my loss rise like color to my cheeks, I marked its passage through artery and nerve; and I remember sitting in my sorrow, looking at the hospital room, at the bed and the dresser and the flowers on the table and at Emily, who, at that moment, was as lifeless and cold for me as the chair itself or the white sheets or the rounded pillow. I remember staring at the design of a knob on a drawer, the bright, glistening, faceted glass, the brass center. Emily's sobs came to me as if from a distance. All sound seemed to be deadened by the room's breathless air. Then at last, I was able to lean forward, able to grip the arms of my chair, able to speak.

"Listen," I said, "you may have what you want. You can divorce me or not divorce me and, either way, I will take care of you. I will give you money, whatever you ask. But I don't want to see you. I don't want to talk to you. For the rest of my life, I don't even want to know if you're alive."

She was silent. She didn't look up. She didn't move her hands from in front of her face.

After a moment, I rose and left the hospital and went to the parking lot and got in my car. I put the key in the ignition lock, but I didn't turn it. I didn't feel I had strength enough to turn it, so I didn't try. I lowered my head until it rested on the rim of the steering wheel and, for a long time, I sat there thinking of Tavean; remembering him and remembering how much I had loved him and knowing the extent of my sorrow now that he was dead.

But life goes on. That is the thing that you have to learn. Whatever grief or pain the world makes you bear, all the others, the people around you, go on living. Life goes on; and, unless you take to bed and lock your door, you are caught up in its current, you have to go on with the business of living, too. Which is, in a gross sort of way, what I did.

There was Anne, of course, and she was once more in mourning and, although she allowed Philip to come to call on her, she did not go out. So for a while, through January and February and March and April, I could leave the office and count on her being there when I got home, count on having a drink with her in the steadily lengthening twilight, count on seeing her—and perhaps Philip too—when I went in to dinner. I had always loved her and she had always been a comfort to me, but never more than in these months following Tavean's death.

I know now that I was a burden to her. She and Philip wanted to be alone and many evenings I sat with them until midnight or after. The conversation became strained sometimes and sometimes Anne was hard pressed to fill our strained silences. For what were we to talk about? What subjects could we pursue that would not lead us sooner or later to the name of Emily or to that of Tavean or to the war that my grandfather had fought in until his death? My days were filled with thoughts of the stock market, but which of us in the den or the library after dinner did not remember the way Tavean and I had sat and drunk and discussed the market in the gloomy nights that came after Nancy's suicide? Indeed, the presence of Philip and Anne and me, sadly together in a lonely house, was a reminder in itself of Tavean's absence. But as bad as it was to remain downstairs, it was worse to go up to bed alone, to sit alone in my sitting room, or to lie awake in the darkness, listening to the sound of the spring wind in the budding trees.

One night I talked to Anne about Emily. We were at dinner and I think I had drunk too much before dinner started. The whiskey had loosened my tongue, I suppose, and sharpened my sadness. I told her how I had been to the hospital and what I had said to Emily and what she had said to me. I told Anne that I had meant what I said, and that I never intended to see Emily again or even talk to her on the telephone.

Anne did not answer at once. She looked at me with her face lifted; the dark eyes, the dark hair, the wide forehead. Then she said, "Do you remember what I told you the night of the accident?"

I didn't at first and then I did. "That I would have to forgive her?"

"That you would have to forgive them," Anne replied.

"I have forgiven Tavean," I said. "That's all I can do. I can never forgive Emily."

She waited a moment. "What are you going to do about Great-grandfather Adams?" she asked.

"Leave him where he is," I said. For I had thought of this. I did not want to see his grave. I did not want to look at the house where he had died or meet the people who lived there.

"Leave him there?" Anne said.

"Yes," I replied. "Because he betrayed me, too, don't you see? He was just like the rest of them."

"Father, Father," she said, "nobody is perfect."

"That's true," I replied, "but I don't see what that has to do with it."

Later, in May, she told me that she had set the date for her marriage to Philip. This news came to me as a shock, for though I had known that she was going to marry, I had thought that she would wait longer because of Tavean's death.

It was Sunday and we were on the terrace. The day was absolutely still, the sky blue and completely cloudless. I remember that I sat and looked out across the lawn at the bright grass, the deep green shadows.

Finally, I said, "My dear, must you be in such a hurry?"
And she said, "Father, I will have to do it sometime."

But why did she have to do it? I thought. Why did she have to marry him at all? For him to die, perhaps to kill himself as Nancy had done? For him to go away with someone else and leave her to endless days and months and years of bitter loneliness?

"You don't have to marry," I said.

"But I want to," she replied softly. "I'm in love with Philip."

"But he may not love you," I said rapidly, cruelly, "he may tire of you, he may . . . "

"Hush!" she said. "Hush!" She got up quickly and grasped my arms and shook me, not hard and not violently, but with great passion. "I love him," she said, "don't you understand that? I love him and I trust him and . . ." She stopped and knelt beside my chair. "Oh, I love him," she said. "I will always love him. I love him better than anything else in the whole world." Then she put her head on my shoulder and began to cry.

So they were married with very little ceremony, with no guest list outside the very closest friends, no dinner before, and no breakfast afterwards. They were pronounced man and wife and Anne came home and changed her clothes and they got in Philip's automobile and drove away.

I stood on the porch with the servants, watching the car move down the driveway, watching the driveway after the car was gone. Then I looked around and the servants were gone too, and I was the only one waiting there with the day quiet all around me, no bird singing, no human voice speaking, and Anne most likely never to return here to live again.

I had invited her and Philip to live with me. There was plenty of room. Judging by the sort of appartments and houses people live in these days, there was room enough in my house for half a dozen families. There were people hired to do the cooking and the cleaning and Philip and Anne would be freed of all domestic responsibility. But they had refused me. Or rather Philip had said nothing and Anne had said no. So now I stood on the quiet porch, staring at the sunlit, empty driveway, wishing for somebody to come and talk to me, have a drink with me, but nobody came and I had the drink alone.

And not only that day and that night, but the next and the next and the next, even after Anne and Philip had returned from their honeymoon. When they got back to Nashville they had me to dinner. But what good was it to spend a few hours in their company, to eat Anne's bad cooking in their little dining room when, like some ancient Cinderella, I would have to return at midnight to my own empty halls? I did not stop loving Anne and I welcomed the opportunity to see her and to see Philip, but I could not understand the way they lived; the apartment when Anne could well afford a house, her insistence on doing her own work when she could well afford servants. I could never quite share their enthusiasm over the articles Philip published in historical journals, and I could never really bear to think about them as two people in love. I knew, of course, that they shared the same bed, that he kissed her when he left for his classes in the morning, and embraced her again when he returned in the afternoon. I knew, but I could not admit to myself that I knew. I did not dare dwell on the feelings they had for each other.

So I lived my lonely life; and my loneliness developed its own design, which was to keep me away from home most of the time. I interested myself in my work as best I could and, usually when I left the office, I would go to the country club and go into the bar and see whom I could find there. I would drink with the golfers and listen to them discuss their scores, or I would drink with the bridge players, or I would drink with the swimmers, or the tennis addicts. I made no distinctions. I would drink with anybody and I would dine with anybody, and what matter if I made a nuisance of myself, and what matter what discussions they had behind my back, what they said about me and Tavean and Emily?

I gave up my pride for the sake of company. But whatever you do, wherever you go, the time to return home must surely come sooner or later. To return alone to an empty house, over and over, night after night, is the nearest thing I know to eternity; and loneliness, which is the sense of love's loss, is the nearest thing on earth to death.

Or, at least, that is the way it seemed to me and that is why, in the fall, I took a trip to Florida. I went because I had to get away, because maybe I had grown tired of the bridge players and the golfers, and maybe on the seashore I could, at least, find some fishermen to talk to. I went because I was tired of drinking in the country club bar and going befuddled home to the house full of memories, full of the remnants of all my old days of joy and sorrow.

I went and rented a suite in a hotel by the ocean. I took in the sun and swam in the surf and kept on drinking.

Late one afternoon, I was sitting at the hotel bar and a blond girl came in and sat down beside me. It is strange what tricks your mind will play, because seeing her out of the corner of my eye, I thought she was Emily. She was not Emily, of course. She was blond all right, and tall, but the shade of her hair was somehow too harsh and the fullness of her hips was too abrupt and across her hips, the white linen dress fit too tightly. But for an instant, I thought she was Emily and I turned on my stool and stared at her in surprise.

"I'm sorry," I said. "I thought you were someone else. I thought I knew you."

"It's all right," she replied, smiling. "I'm Helen Williams. Now you do know me."

And, of course, it is not that easy. Of course, any fool should have known. But there is no fool like an old fool and no old fool like a lonely old fool. I bought her a couple of drinks and took her to dinner. Looking back, it seems to me that we spent our time that night in endless movement, in going from bar to nightclub and from nightclub to roadhouse, and always on the table or the counter before me, there was a drink that I didn't remember ordering, but which I drank to the bottom just the same. I remember how quickly the time passed, how it was nine o'clock and ten o'clock and then twelve o'clock and one o'clock; and I remember strangely little about Helen Williams, but I recollect very well the fondness I felt for her. I held her hand and danced with her, and she sat close to me when we drove from one saloon to another.

It was very nice to have a woman beside me again and to smell a woman's perfume and to feel the fine, soft touch of a woman's hair against my cheek.

Late that night, so late that I had lost track of the time, I parked on the beach. I stopped the car in the darkness and turned off the radio, so there was only the sound of the surf breaking, and between the waves, the sound of Helen Williams' breathing and the sound in my ears of my own beating heart. I put my arm around her and kissed her, and a woman's kiss is something that you cannot remember, not really, for the tactile senses have no recollection. You know that to kiss is good and pleasant, but that is the knowledge of the mind and the good kiss comes as a joyful surprise, a rediscovery. I kissed her and felt her body close to mine. I knew that this was what I wanted most of all, this was the antidote for all my loneliness, this was what I would like to have for the rest of my days.

"Helen," I said, "I love you."

"You're sweet," she replied. "I think you're nice, too."

"Marry me," I said. "Listen. I've got plenty of money. Marry me and come home with me to Tennessee."

"We'll talk about it tomorrow," she said.

"No," I said petulantly. I was feeling angry—the whiskey anger that comes suddenly and without warning. "Talk about it now. I want you to marry me."

"All right," she said. "I'll marry you, Horatio."

And I think I had another drink, one more to celebrate my engagement, but I can't be sure, for I recall very little that happened after that. I have a vague memory of Helen driving the car, of waking up and seeing her profile in the dash light. I seem to remember, too, going into the hotel, being helped in by some strange man who got the key to the suite out of my pocket.

The next morning, when I was awakened by the telephone, I was lying on a couch in the sitting room fully clothed. I did not move at once. My head hurt so fearfully that I did not dare lift it off the cushion. There was a crick in my neck and my mouth was dry and I felt slightly nauseated. But I had to do something to stop the painful noise of the telephone. Or rather, I had to try to do something, for the first effort I made was unsuccessful. I rose to a sitting position and sat there sweating and trembling.

At last, the telephone stopped ringing. I got up, dizzy, staggering, and made it to the bathroom and got a drink of water. I took some aspirin and kept on drinking water, spilling it sometimes, because my hand was shaking so much and, after a while, the water was cool on my stomach and my stomach felt full, but I was still thirsty. I went back into the sitting room and took off my coat and my tie and shirt and sat down in a chair. Then the telephone rang again and I answered it.

"Mr. Adams?" a man's voice said, "are you the Mr. Adams from Nashville, Tennessee?"

I told him I was.

"This is the police department," he said. "We've got your car. We've got the people who stole it."

I tried to tell him my car had not been stolen, but he knew better. He had the car all right, and he had Helen Williams, and there was a man involved, too. The man had been driving when the police stopped them for speeding. There were Tennessee plates on the automobile, but the man had a Florida license. The police looked in the glove compartment and found the title which bore my name.

I told the officer that I would come to headquarters later in the morning, and then I put down the phone and felt in my pocket and my billfold was gone. My watch was missing from my wrist. Somebody had even taken my tie clasp and my cufflinks. It didn't take a genius to figure out who that somebody was.

I was sick—sick with a hangover and sick from shame. My memory started working, bringing back the events of the night before, and I began talking out loud to myself in my utter embarrassment.

"I don't know what I'm going to do," I said, and I wasn't thinking about the missing cufflinks or the watch or the car or the money. I said, "I made a fool of myself and I don't know what I'm going to do."

I sat miserably in my chair, my head throbbing, the bright light of the morning hurting my eyes. I wanted to think about anything in the world except the way I had gone out with that tramp of a woman and sat with her in the car and asked her to marry me. I knew I would have to go to the police station or else the police would come to the hotel in search of me. I would have to go and talk to the officers and maybe I would have to see the woman there. I did not think I could stand this and it did not seem right that I should have to look at her again.

Oh, I thought, how could my life be brought to this? How could fate do this to me, and I getting on toward old age now, in a few years I would be sixty. Nancy, I thought, if Nancy had not killed herself. Or Emily. Or Tavean. Or even Anne. After all the others had proved false, even Anne might have saved me if she had really tried. "They don't care about me," I said out loud. "None of them ever cared about me."

But this wasn't true. I sat and tried to make myself believe it was true. I said to myself over and over again, *Nobody ever loved me.* But it wouldn't work. I knew that they had loved me, that all of them had loved me. And I knew that I had loved all of them, but something had gone wrong. Something, but I didn't know what.

I ordered some coffee and drank a little bit of it. Then I took a shower and shaved and had another cup and went down and cashed a check and took a cab to the police station. I hoped that when I got there, if they made me see Helen Williams at all, they would put her in a line up like they do in the movies and on television. I could pick her out of the line up from my seat in the darkness and the lights would keep her from recognizing me. But this is not the way it happened.

The officer, a plain-clothes man with a wide, tanned face, took me first to a parking lot where I identified my car. Then we went to a little office. I sat down and Helen Williams and a man in a sport shirt were brought there, I suppose from the jail. I only glanced at the man, and I did not want to look at Helen Williams, but I could not help looking at her. I kept hoping that her features would soften, that some change in her expression or even movement of her head would make her appear a little kinder, a little nicer. If she were really beautiful, maybe I could start forgiving myself for what I had done.

But she wasn't beautiful. Her eyes were very small and

hard and she wore too much lipstick. In the full light of day, her complexion was rather coarse. She stood with her legs spread apart, her weight on one foot, her hip stuck out. She regarded me with a kind of scared contempt that resembled hatred.

"You know her?" the officer said.

"Yes," I said quietly, my eyes averted.

"She and the boy here roll you last night, Mr. Adams? Did they steal anything from you?"

The room was very silent. They all waited. I didn't look up. "No," I said at last. "They didn't rob me."

"They had your car," the officer said. "They were stealing that, weren't they?"

"No," I said again. "I lent it to her."

"May I see your driver's license, Mr. Adams?"

I reached automatically toward my pocket and then I remembered. "I'm sorry," I said. "I lost it. I lost my billfold."

"Yeah," the officer said gloomily. Then he said, "Mr. Adams, we'd like to stop this sort of thing down here. We want people to have a good time without getting taken. Why don't you help us? Not a bit of this will get in the papers. Not even down here. You won't even have to wait on a long court docket. We can get a quick trial and put these two away."

Again there was the moment of expectant silence.

And again I said, "No. It wasn't their fault. They didn't do anything, not anything at all to me."

And that was true. They hadn't done anything to me. This time, what had happened to me, I had done to myself. *I did it,* I said driving back to the hotel, *I did it,* I repeated over and over. *But I'm not going to do anything like this again. I'm going home and I'm going to stop all this drinking. And if I've got to be alone for the rest of my life, then I will learn to live with loneliness.* I was going to do this, because I was Horatio Adams. I wasn't going to let Horatio Adams turn into an old lecher, a debauched relic who had lost all self-respect.

Hungover, guilt-ridden as I was, I left for Nashville that very day. I had a bottle of whiskey in my hotel room, but I did not take it with me. I did not have a drink on the road, and I did not have one when I got home, tired as I was from the two days' journey. The next night I went to dinner with Anne and Philip, and when Philip offered me a martini, I told him no thank you. I hadn't sworn off. I hadn't given it up forever. But I figured I had to take a while to get my bearings and to stay off liquor for a while to prove that I could.

When I turned down the drink, Anne and Philip were surprised. They asked me what was the matter, and I told them there was no trouble. They sat holding their own glasses and the conversation died. We sat and looked at each other and heard the traffic noises from the street. I lighted a cigarette and watched the smoke drift. Philip regarded Anne with a tender gaze and they smiled at each other. Then Philip turned the same silly smile on me and said, "You'll have to have a drink, Horatio. We're celebrating."

"Celebrating what?" I said.

"Us," Anne replied foolishly, "the natural processes. We're going to have a baby."

"What?" I said.

"A baby," Philip said, rising out of his chair. "Think of that, Horatio! A grandchild for you! If it's a boy, by God, we'll name him after Bedford Forrest!"

He did not mean anything by this. I should not have expected him to be ever-mindful of my sorrow. But for me, this reference to General Forrest, this juxtaposition of the past with the future, brought into sharp and immediate focus all the pains and losses of my life. Or maybe it wasn't what Philip said. Maybe it was simply the knowledge that the child was coming, which reminded me of the child that I had lost. Or maybe it was not this either. Maybe it was simply the idea of youth, the thought of how much time this baby would have before it to repair whatever mistakes it made, to find love and to keep love, as I hoped to God Anne and Philip would be able to keep it. I had always wanted Anne to be happy. I had wanted it until the wanting had become a habit, like smoking or sleeping or brushing your teeth, so I did not think about it very often unless something threatened it. But it seemed to me now that the greatest threat to happiness was the mere existence of happiness, the joy that you could never be sure of, the ecstasy that might be taken from you at any hour. I wanted suddenly to warn Anne and Philip. To say, *Be careful, be very careful. Always love each other. Always love the child. Don't ever lose anything. Don't let life take anything away.*

But then it occurred to me that I had been as careful as a man could be and life had deprived me of almost everything. Maybe being careful wasn't the right answer. I didn't know.

I had the drink, but I didn't stay to dinner. I couldn't.

I spoke to them as gently as I could. I congratulated them and I apologized for leaving, but I had to get out of the house. I had to go somewhere and decide what I was going to do.

I'll go to the club, I thought. But I knew that that would be starting down the same old path that had taken me to Florida and to Helen Williams, so I went home instead. I went in to the bar and, almost without thinking, I poured a drink and I had that one, but I didn't take any more.

I didn't have anything else to drink, but what then? What was I going to accomplish just sitting there looking at the walls? All right, I thought, Anne's married and she's going to have a baby. And she can bring the baby to see me on Sunday afternoons. It can play in the yard and I can play with it, or sit on the porch and watch it and talk to Anne. In between times, I can go to my office and maybe I can develop some hobby. Maybe I can collect something at night or write a book. But this was evasion. I knew it was evasion, and I knew that I was going to have to face up, sooner or later, to the truth of my life. I suppose I didn't know what the truth was, but it was apparently something more than just what had happened to me, because I had been thinking about that for a long time without reaching any conclusion, without learning anything, without finding peace. Yes, I put it that way to myself. I used that word, peace, without knowing any better than anybody else in this vale of tears what peace means, what it would look like if it came and sat down in the chair across from me. Maybe it would have been better if

I had said I was looking for reality. I don't know. But I was looking for something, and that for a fact.

And maybe to find truth or reality or the way to peace—whatever it is that you in your man-foolishness are looking for—you have to go somewhere. In the old time, so the poets tell us, you went down to the underworld, down to the land where the dead had gone, and you came back knowing something you had never known before. Well, if there was an underworld I could go to, a land of the dead where I could gain admittance, it was an antebellum house thirty miles south of Nashville, a few miles south of the town of Van Buren where once a battle had been fought. Now, at this time of night, when the traffic had thinned out, you could make it in less than an hour. I got in my car and drove to Adams' Rest.

I went in and turned up the heat and switched on the lights in every room. I went and looked in every room; I made the tour. I had thought that the house would be full of ghosts. I had expected to hear voices whispering to me from the shadows. I had counted on seeing some insubstantial figure flit out of sight around a corner at my approach. But here there were no ghosts. The house was empty.

I went to the bedroom behind the library and all I saw there was the furniture of the room. Tavean had been here once, but Tavean was not here now, and he would never be here again, no matter how long I stood and looked and waited. I walked up the stairs to my own bedroom, and I thought, this is where Emily packed her bags to leave me. She passed through that door, she moved down that hall, she descended the steps and . . . And what? Was Tavean waiting for her, looking up at her, watching in gladness as she came into his view? I tried to answer this question. I tried to imagine how it had been, but I would never know. There were only the rooms, the vacant rooms, the beds and the chests and the carpets and the drapes, and I among them, a palpable, living man, no ghost yet, though some day I would be.

A little disappointed, I made my way to the living room. I lit the fire that was laid there and sat down near the hearth. I sat for a while and watched the flames and then I looked up and there above the mantelpiece was my grandfather's portrait. I spoke to it.

I said, "You're dead."

And that being indisputably true, he did not answer.

I thought about Grandfather being dead and, in a way, the thought was like a new thought. It was as if my heart had never really believed it before, though my mind had known it. I looked at the picture again and I said, without rancor, but without sympathy, too, "You played hell that night in that lady's house near Columbia."

And he had done that, all right. He had played hell for both of us. He had betrayed me fifty years before I was born, but I had got even. I had betrayed him too, I had exposed him for what he was. There would be no more Confederate flags set up in his memory by the gentle, aging ladies of the U.D.C.

I had got even but, oh, what it had cost me. So maybe Anne was right, after all. Maybe you couldn't go on hating. Maybe you had to forgive. "All right," I said. "I'll forgive you. I'll send Rathbone down to the Dedman place to get your body. I'll bury you out here like I meant to do all along."

But what about me? I thought. *Who's going to forgive me?* I looked at the picture. *Not you. You're gone. You're past forgiving.* I remembered that when I had gone to see Emily in the hospital; I had said to her, *Why did you do it?* And she had replied, *I don't know. Why did you?*

Had I done it? Was it Tavean's death that I had to be forgiven for? Or, to look further back, was it my fault that Nancy had killed herself? Yes, it must have been, at least in a way. In a way, I was responsible and what matter if I were not wholly, singly responsible? What matter if each of them had had some responsibility, too? I shared the guilt of all the past. I shared even in the guilt of my grandfather. Except I was worse than he was. I had proved that by what I had done in Florida.

Nancy, Nancy, I thought. *Tavean, Tavean. Oh, my dears, I am sorry. I am very sorry.* But, of course, they didn't hear me anymore than the portrait of my grandfather had heard me. They might be able to hear Anne with her prayers and candles, but they could not hear me.

Among those whom I had wronged the most, only Emily was left alive and what could I do for her more than what I was doing? She was so very young. She still had so much of life left before her. I could at least make her get a divorce. I could free her and give her some money and, perhaps, she could forget about the old man who once had loved her. *Who still loves her,* I thought, and the thought did not even surprise me. I guess I had never stopped loving her, even in the bitterest moments after the death of Tavean.

I'll set her free, I said to myself. She hadn't asked for a divorce, but I would give her one anyway. And I would tell her to stop worrying. I would do like Anne said, I would forgive her. And after that, I would go on living alone and I would get used to living alone, because maybe, if you try hard enough, you can get used to anything.

So I went to see Emily the next day. She was living with her mother and I found when I got there that I had almost forgotten how beautiful she was or, at least, I had not prepared myself to see her beauty. I had come to give her up, to send her finally and irrevocably away from me, but I had not steeled myself properly. I almost faltered.

"You are looking well," I said. "My dear, you are very . . ." and I broke off in time. I had almost said lovely.

"How are you?" she asked.

I told her I was well.

Then came the silence which is the worst kind of silence of all; the terrible, heart-rending deadness that falls over estranged intimacy. Once we had known love's full consummation, once we had had no secret thoughts. Now we could find no word to fill the vacancy between us.

"Would you like some coffee?" she said at last.

"No," I replied, "I have come to tell you something."

She said nothing.

"I have come to tell you to quit worrying," I said. "Forget about what has happened. Forget about me. I should never have asked you to marry me. I was too old for you."

"No," she said. "It wasn't that. Age made no difference."

"Yes," I replied, "you're right. It wasn't age. It was me. It was the way I felt about life. I don't know how to put it exactly. I guess a part of it was that I couldn't bear happiness."

"Why not?" she said leaning forward. "I wondered about that, Horatio. What happened to us? Why did things work out the way they did?"

"Why?" I said. "Nobody ever really knows why. There are a thousand reasons for every turn of every day." I pondered this a while, knowing it was true. Thinking that not only did God know about the fall of the sparrow, but that only the mind of God could know all the reasons why the sparrow fell.

"My dear," I said, "all you can do is admit your own part in things. That's what I'm trying to do now. I want to make it up to you somehow. I want you to be free, so you can start over again, so you can . . ." But I couldn't get the rest of it out; I couldn't bring myself to say marry someone else.

"A divorce?" Emily said.

I nodded. "Yes. For you."

"I don't want a divorce, Horatio," she said wearily. "The only reason for me to get a divorce would be to marry again. And I think I have had enough of marriage. I think I have had enough to last me the rest of my life."

I wished that I could call it all back. I wished that none of it had ever happened. I wished that I had never come into her life to embitter her this way.

"My dear," I said softly, "don't say that. You are young and I have wronged you greatly. If you marry again, you will likely suffer again, but it is worth it, Emily. That's what I didn't understand. There is always the pain that comes with the happiness, but if you will accept the happiness it is worth the pain. Oh," I said, "don't be like me. Don't end up like me, old and alone and not worth anything to anybody."

She was silent for a long time. "Can I help you?" she said finally. "Do you want me now?"

Out of pity? I thought. Do I want her if she comes to me out of pity? Do I want her to return to me not because she loves me purely, but because she doesn't want to see me suffer anymore?

I considered this and then I thought, yes. Yes. Because pity is a kind of love. And nothing in the world is ever pure. Not even love. Not even joy. Not even sorrow.

Voices of the South

Hamilton Basso
   The View from Pompey's Head
Richard Bausch
   Real Presence
   Take Me Back
Doris Betts
   The Astronomer and Other Stories
   The Gentle Insurrection
Sheila Bosworth
   Almost Innocent
   Slow Poison
David Bottoms
   Easter Weekend
Erskine Caldwell
   Poor Fool
Fred Chappell
   The Gaudy Place
   The Inkling
   It Is Time, Lord
Kelly Cherry
   Augusta Played
Vicki Covington
   Bird of Paradise
Ellen Douglas
   A Family's Affairs
   A Lifetime Burning
   The Rock Cried Out
Percival Everett
   Suder
Peter Feibleman
   The Daughters of Necessity
   A Place Without Twilight
George Garrett
   Do, Lord, Remember Me
   An Evening Performance
Marianne Gingher
   Bobby Rex's Greatest Hit
Shirley Ann Grau
   The House on Coliseum Street
   The Keepers of the House
Barry Hannah
   The Tennis Handsome

Donald Hays
   The Dixie Association
William Humphrey
   Home from the Hill
   The Ordways
Mac Hyman
   No Time For Sergeants
Madison Jones
   A Cry of Absence
Nancy Lemann
   Lives of the Saints
   Sportman's Paradise
Willie Morris
   The Last of the Southern Girls
Louis D. Rubin, Jr.
   The Golden Weather
Evelyn Scott
   The Wave
Lee Smith
   The Last Day the Dogbushes Bloomed
Elizabeth Spencer
   The Salt Line
   The Voice at the Back Door
Max Steele
   Debby
Walter Sullivan
   The Long, Long Love
Allen Tate
   The Fathers
Peter Taylor
   The Widows of Thornton
Robert Penn Warren
   Band of Angels
   Brother to Dragons
   World Enough and Time
Walter White
   Flight
Joan Williams
   The Morning and the Evening
   The Wintering
Thomas Wolfe
   The Web and the Rock